"You're my employee, not my lover."

"You hired me to be both," he couldn't resist pointing out.

Tess didn't let him get away with it. "I hired you to *play* the part of my lover. That doesn't mean you're supposed to grab and kiss your boss. Or is that standard operating procedure with you?"

He eyed her with amused frankness. "I believe you're the first employer I've ever grabbed and kissed." An eyebrow lifted in question. "Are you firing me?"

"I'm willing to let it go this once." A hint of steel threaded her voice. "But I won't agree to your terms...."

Marriages made in moments!

Finding the perfect partner isn't easy....
Enter the Cupid Committee! Quietly, secretly,
but very successfully, this group of anonymous
romantics has set hundreds of unsuspecting
singles on the path to matrimony....

Take Tess, Emma and Raine. Three best friends
who made a pact: if they're still single when they
turn thirty, they have permission to play matchmaker
for each other! But they have no idea that Cupid is
about to deliver a lightning strike....

Three women, three unexpected romances in:

August 2001: The Provocative Proposal (#3663)

Coming in 2002:
The Whirlwind Wedding
The Baby Bombshell

DAY LECLAIRE

The Provocative Proposal

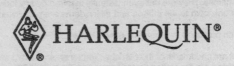

TORONTO • NEW YORK • LONDON
AMSTERDAM • PARIS • SYDNEY • HAMBURG
STOCKHOLM • ATHENS • TOKYO • MILAN • MADRID
PRAGUE • WARSAW • BUDAPEST • AUCKLAND

To family, who mean the world to me.

ISBN 0-373-03663-9

THE PROVOCATIVE PROPOSAL

First North American Publication 2001.

PROLOGUE

"PLEASE address the Committee."

Tess Lonigan stepped into the splash of light that broke the darkness of the room. "Is this the matchmaking committee?"

Her question prompted a rustle of papers and a number of whispered comments. Finally a voice she recognized replied. "It is. You have a request to make?"

She struggled to keep a straight face. Her brother was doing his best to disguise his voice with a phony Southern accent—not that it was working. All it did was make her want to laugh. "I have two friends I'd like you to match. The first is Emma Palmer from San Francisco. The other is Raine Featherstone, a Texan."

"They want this match?" he questioned.

"No. But I've been authorized to make it for them."

"Okay, we'll bite." Thank goodness Seth had finally dropped the ridiculous accent. "How have you been authorized if they're not interested in a match?"

"The three of us made an agreement years ago. If any of us reached age thirty and hadn't found our soul mate, the others were assigned to find him."

More rustle of papers and more conversation. She wished she could see who the various members of this committee were, but they'd arranged the lighting to prevent that. Great. She'd stepped into a *film noir*, complete with spotlighted interrogation, a secret committee and a redheaded damsel in distress. She bit back another grin. Okay, so maybe she wasn't really a damsel in distress,

5

but it sounded good. Now all she needed was a tough-guy protagonist and the cast would be complete.

Right on cue a new voice spoke up. "Interesting agreement. Are you sure it wasn't a joke on their part?"

She didn't recognize the speaker, but his words grated, the intonation far gruffer than her brother's. "It might have been," she admitted with a shrug.

"So why should we turn this joke against them?"

"Against them?" Tess folded her arms across her chest. "Is that what you think marriage is, a joke between two combatants? What gives? I thought you guys were a bunch of modern day Cupids."

"We match only those ready for marriage."

"In that case, my friends are perfect choices. Not only are they ready for marriage—whether they realize it or not—but at least one of them has the perfect man sitting on her doorstep."

"Then why does she need us?"

"Because she can't see how perfect this man is. To be honest, both my friends require a little nudge from some helpful Cupids. It should be a snap for you guys. All you have to do is send in your—" Her brow wrinkled as she struggled to come up with the appropriate word. "Oh, right. Your Instigator. It shouldn't take him any time at all to get the job done."

Seth groaned.

"How do you know about the Instigator?" Mr. Tough Guy demanded.

She assumed her most innocent expression. Of course, having reached the ripe age of thirty, herself, playing the dewy-eyed ingénue was a bit of a stretch. "Gee, was that a secret?"

"Dammit, Tess!" Seth interrupted. "Of course, it was a secret."

She smiled sweetly. "Then I guess big brothers shouldn't have private conversations where their little sisters can overhear them."

"Enough." With that one word, Mr. Tough Guy achieved instant silence. Tess was impressed. She wouldn't mind having that effect on people at work. "We'll grant your request on one condition."

Uh-oh. "Which is?"

"This Committee operates in secret. We prefer to keep it that way."

"That might be wise," she muttered. "The idea of a bunch of crazy Cupids running around instigating love affairs is a little tough to swallow."

"You might be interested to know that we have a perfect record," Seth retorted. "Three hundred and twenty-two perfectly matched couples enjoying wedded bliss. Why, we've instigated more marriages than... Than..."

"Then those Cinderella Ball people and their Fairytale Weddings," another voice inserted.

Mr. Tough Guy cleared his throat. "To be honest, I believe we're currently tied with them."

"I get the idea," Tess interrupted. Typical committee. They couldn't even agree among themselves. "How's this? You ensure wedded bliss for my two friends and I'll keep quiet about your little organization. Is it a deal?"

"It's a deal," Seth concurred.

Apparently, no further discussion was necessary. The door behind Tess opened and the circle of light surrounding her vanished. Okay, she could take a hint. They wanted her to leave? She'd leave. Only one thing gave her pause as she walked out the door. She couldn't help wondering if she'd made a terrible mistake.

"Well?" Seth asked the minute she'd left the room.

Shadoe stepped from the darkness. "How much does she know?" His rumbly voice sat well with both his name and appearance.

"About our plans to match her? Nothing. Her visit today is purely coincidental. My fault I'm afraid. She overheard a phone conversation and decided to take advantage of the situation in order to help her friends."

"But she knows of the Instigator."

"She doesn't know Shayde's name or that he's been assigned to find her a husband."

"How will she react when she finds out what we've done?"

"She won't take it well. Not well at all." Seth grinned. "But by then I'm hoping it'll be far too late. She's going to get happily-ever-after whether she wants it or not."

Shadoe nodded. "In that case, we'll proceed. I'll call my brother and set events in motion. Once we have Tess settled we can turn our attention to her friends."

CHAPTER ONE

HE CAME with the night, embodying its most visceral qualities and stirring something deeply feminine within her.

Tess Lonigan sat behind her safe, practical desk and fought to remain rational in the face of a man who could only be described as dark, mysterious and dangerous. Very dangerous. He stood on the far side of the room and for a long moment they simply stared at each other. The feeble light cast from the lamp on her desk failed to penetrate his cloak of shadows, allowing him to melt into his surroundings. Of course, his all-black attire and ebony hair didn't help, nor the stillness with which he held himself. Worse were his eyes. She couldn't make out the precise color, but they were the only thing about him that escaped his mask of darkness. They flickered like starlight, the power of his gaze and unwavering directness more disconcerting than anything she'd ever seen before.

Dark, mysterious and dangerous.

The words repeated in a nerve-racking refrain and a small frown pulled her brows together. They weren't qualities she admired. How could Jeanne at the employment agency think this man would be appropriate for what she had in mind? Realizing she was on the verge of snapping her pen in half, she carefully returned it to the crisp white blotter protecting her desk and reached an instant decision. No. This man would never do.

Desperate to end the silent battle of wills, she gestured

for him to approach. Normally, she'd have stood and shook hands, offering a warm smile of welcome. But instinct warned that would be a mistake. Her worst mistake, though, had been scheduling this meeting for after-hours. Everything felt more intense and exaggerated when wrapped within night's powerful embrace. Not that she'd had any other choice than to schedule the appointment for this late. She didn't dare let anyone know the reason she'd decided to hire outside help.

He moved forward, not quite slipping free of the shadows. They continued to drape him like the wispy vestiges of some princely mantle. "You requested my services?" he asked.

Even his voice struck her as wrong. Instead of smooth and polished, it rasped, his every word snagging her full attention whether she wanted to give it to him or not. It reminded her vaguely of Mr. Tough Guy from the Cupid Committee. Only this man's voice was slightly deeper and far rougher. "You were sent by the employment agency?" she demanded.

He inclined his head and the subdued lighting caught in his dark hair. It fell to his collar in rebellious waves, no doubt an outward expression of the persona he concealed behind an impenetrable mask. "Jeanne chose me. I'm the most suitable candidate for what you have in mind."

An intense wave of vulnerability caught her by surprise and prompted a cold briskness completely out of character. "She couldn't have looked very hard."

He took the criticism without comment, though she noted a spark of amusement gleam in his eyes. They truly were odd eyes, almost silver in color and disconcerting in their directness. "Try checking my qualifications before making assumptions."

She forced her lips into a smile of agreement. "Excellent point. Though considering one of the qualifications is how well we get along, that may not take much time."

He didn't respond, turning an assessing gaze on both her and the office. If he was hoping to read her character by analyzing her appearance or surroundings, he'd fail miserably. She'd designed her office in a color and style meant to relax her clients, while dressing in a manner intended to come across as friendly and nonthreatening. Both were carefully calculated and had nothing whatsoever to do with her true nature.

"Do you always make snap judgments about people?" he asked as soon as he'd completed his appraisal.

She matched his uncompromising bluntness. "No."

His full attention fell on her and it took every ounce of self-possession to keep from reacting to the acuteness of that look. "But in my case...?" He allowed the statement to trail off and waited.

To her surprise she found herself answering, which only annoyed her all the more. She preferred keeping her own council, explaining herself and justifying her opinions as little as possible. But there was something about this man, something that forced a response. "You're not the sort of man I'd marry."

Silence reigned for an uncomfortable moment. "Perhaps we should start over," he suggested mildly. "You're Tess Lonigan?"

She nodded.

"I'm Shayde. I'm here for a job interview." He stressed the word "job."

"Shayde?" she managed to get out. "Is that your first name or last?"

"It's all of my name."

He stated it with such quiet conviction that there was nothing left for her to say. It was an odd name, and yet it suited him. He looked like a man of shade and shadow. "Please sit down, Mr.—"

"Just Shayde," came the gentle reminder.

"Right. Please have a seat."

Out of sheer desperation, she shifted some papers from one side of her desk to the other. It gave her a moment to conceal her reaction to him. This was ridiculous. She'd never had trouble interviewing potential employees before. Why should this time be any different? And yet, it was. *He* was. She sensed a dangerously masculine quality enveloping him, a dark ambience that offered a subtle threat she perceived on an instinctive level. It called to everything female within her, humming through her in persistent waves, a forbidden temptation she shouldn't recognize, let alone respond to. And yet, she wanted to respond, to answer this most primitive of calls. Male pursuing female. Push battling pull. Woman yielding to man.

Don't forget what's at stake, came the pointed reminder. The single thought proved a sobering influence. After an endless minute, Tess looked up, able to meet Shayde's regard with something approaching equanimity. "What details has Jeanne given you about the job?"

"She said you needed an escort to accompany you to business functions."

"I'm not interested in a professional escort," she explained.

Something ominous flashed in his eyes. "That's good since I have nothing in common with that breed of man."

"Then what are you?" The question escaped before she could prevent it. It was a painfully honest demand, one that cut straight to the heart of the matter. It was also a dead giveaway, the sort of question a woman would ask, rather than an employer. A single knowing look from Shayde had Tess scrambling to alter the slant of her query. "I mean, what's your professional background?"

"I have a résumé, if that'll reassure you. It'll show that I have an eclectic business background, varied enough to hold my own in most conversations. And Jeanne has checked my references. They're impeccable."

"She wouldn't have sent you if they weren't."

"You might keep that in mind during the selection process." He leaned back in the chair. He moved with a lazy grace that conflicted dramatically with the underlying tension of a man poised to react to the least provocation. "Why don't you tell me a little about your requirements for the job. In fact, why don't you explain what you need and why."

She hadn't planned to go into so much detail, not until she'd selected the right candidate for the job. But something about the sheer force of Shayde's personality compelled a response. "The company I work for is called Altruistics, Inc. Ever hear of us?"

"You solicit money on behalf of various charitable organizations, don't you?"

"Right. We're a privately owned business that has successfully raised millions for cancer research, homeless shelters, drug abuse programs. You name a good cause and we've found people with nice, deep pockets who can be persuaded to dip into them and help out."

"Why do I sense a 'but' coming?"

She smiled. "Maybe because there is one. Ready?"

"Hit me."

"I'm up for a promotion."

He took a minute to assess her comment before asking the next logical question. "A promotion you'll receive depending on...what?"

"Depending on my business success over the next two weeks."

"Intriguing." He regarded her with intense interest. "How is your success determined?"

She might as well explain it all. Something told her that Shayde wouldn't accept anything less than absolute frankness. "We have potential benefactors that we refer to as the 'Impossibles.' In the past they've always been thought impossible to successfully solicit."

"In other words, they have their own favorite charities and aren't interested in funneling any of their spare cash in your direction."

She nodded. "That doesn't stop us from trying."

"I assume you have two weeks in which to turn one of the Impossibles."

His shrewdness impressed her. "You've got it. Next week we're throwing a huge cancer benefit. That evening, the president of the company will assign me a client."

A small smile touched his mouth. "And the challenge begins."

"Right. Unfortunately, I have three strikes against me before I even begin." She picked up the pen once more and tapped the pristine blotter with it. "At thirty, I'm considered on the young side for this promotion. I suspect that's why I've been asked to turn an Impossible."

"Should I assume that the second strike is that you have competition for the job?"

"Yes." She kept her voice as neutral as possible. "There's another woman who's approached my boss about it. She's a bit older. Her children have all left the nest and she's hungry to advance her career. Very hungry.''

"You said there were three strikes. What's the final one?''

She hesitated. "I'm not married.''

"I gather Mr. Lonigan is no longer in the picture?''

"He died nine years ago.''

Was that compassion she read in his gaze? With his skill at concealing his reactions, she had trouble telling. But she thought she caught a softening in his silvery regard. "I gather we've gotten to the reason I'm sitting here.''

He didn't phrase it as a question and she acknowledged his accurate assessment of the situation with a quick nod. "Yes.''

"Tell me why your marital status is a factor in the promotion.''

Time for a little tiptoeing around some of the more distressing complications she faced. "My job requires a lot of social interaction. If I get this promotion, it'll require even more. I can usually handle it without any problem.''

"Let me guess... That changed recently.''

Tess formulated her answer with care. "I've discovered the advantage of having an escort on the odd occasion.''

Shayde's eyebrow flicked upward. "That's it? That's all you're willing to say?''

"Yes.'' There wasn't any point in explaining how this decision had been brought forcibly home to her. "I need an escort, plain and simple. And I need him in time for the cancer benefit.''

"The question is...why?'' He mulled it over—not

that it took him long to come up with the answer. "I assume that as a single woman you're in the awkward position of entertaining both clients and donors on your own."

His insight was unnerving. "It's not often a problem," she responded.

"Unless someone decides you're part of the offer."

"Yes." So far she'd managed to avoid that particular complication. But that could change depending on the manner of man Dick Smith turned out to be.

"I gather I'm your solution?" He drummed his fingers on the arm of his chair, the first outward reaction he'd allowed himself so far. "You want me to assume spousal duties?"

His phrasing made Tess stir in discomfort. "I suppose that's one way of putting it. It's a temporary position," she added swiftly. "It will only last until the promotion has been decided."

"And what will you do if you get the promotion? It doesn't sound like this situation will go away anytime soon."

"That's my problem."

He started to say more. After a brief hesitation, he inclined his head. "Fair enough. Since you'd rather not go into specifics, perhaps we should discuss my duties. What do you want from me?"

"As I indicated, I'll need an escort to various business functions. I also need someone who's able to accompany me to whatever social engagements I'm required to attend." She ticked off the possibilities. "Dinner. Parties. Everything from black tie to jeans and T-shirts, or anything in between."

"There's more, isn't there?"

How did he do it? She'd known people who could

read situations with amazing accuracy. But his abilities went far beyond that. She forced herself to answer with a frankness that didn't come naturally. "I have to convince people that we're a committed couple."

"Lovers."

She didn't flinch from the word, though it took an impressive amount of control not to. Instead, she kept her gaze locked on his. "I want them to believe our relationship is serious enough that we're contemplating marriage. That's why I said you wouldn't do. You're not the type of man I'd marry."

For the briefest of moments the mask slipped and his expression opened to her. He'd taken her words as a challenge, which she hadn't intended at all. Great. He was *that* type. Tell the man he couldn't have or do something and he was hell-bent to prove you wrong.

"Are you certain I'm not your type?" he asked.

"Positive."

"What makes you so sure?"

"Experience," she said crisply. "You're nothing like my late husband."

That stopped him. But then, that had been her intention. "You had a good marriage?"

"It was wonderful." She fought to keep her emotions in check, to keep from revealing the devastation she'd felt when she'd lost Robert. "But far too brief."

"I'm sorry," he said. There was no mistaking his sincerity. "That must make your current situation all the more difficult."

If only he'd stop staring at her as though he could see straight through to her soul. His words had taken on a gentle quality—at least, as gentle as his gruff voice would allow—and it upset her for some odd reason. It was totally unlike her husband's polished tones, and yet instinct had her reacting to the sound with a disquieting amount of trust. Tess shook her head in silent denial. She must be losing what small scrap of common sense she still retained.

He was waiting for her reply and she dismissed his concern with a quick wave of her hand. The movement came across as disjointed rather than natural and she spared him a quick look. Had he picked up on it? Probably, knowing him. "How I feel about the situation isn't important. Besides, I don't think the few weeks we'll be working together will be difficult at all."

"And why is that?"

"Because we're going to keep everything simple. Our relationship will be business only. Nothing personal, got it?"

"I think you're underestimating what's involved."

She lifted a shoulder in a negligent shrug. "How hard will it be to get through a few business dinners?"

"A few dinners? Is that all you think it'll take?" His mouth curved into a smile rife with irony. "Do you have any idea of the level of intimacy we'll need to fake in order to accomplish what you have in mind?"

"Intimacy won't factor into our relationship." She was already talking as though she'd chosen him for the job, and she hastened to correct the erroneous impression. "It won't factor into the relationship of the person I select."

He released his breath in a quiet laugh. It was as unsettling as everything else about him, the sound disturbingly masculine and sandpaper rough, grating in the most delicious ways. "Don't kid yourself. Women, in particular, will sense the truth." He fixed her with a questioning look. "Can't you? Don't you sense on an instinctive level when a couple is intimately involved?"

She ignored his question. "I doubt it'll be that difficult," she maintained stubbornly. "It's not like we'll be around any particular group of people for any length of time. As long as I'm able to establish a comfortable rapport with the man I hire, people will buy the relationship."

"A comfortable rapport." He weighed the description for a moment. "I gather you don't consider me satisfactory in that department."

He didn't phrase it as a question, so she didn't bother moderating her response. "No."

Shayde fell silent, but she sensed an underlying amusement. His eyes gleamed behind a dark fringe of lashes and the creases on either side of his mouth deepened. "Why don't you tell me what you want in a man."

"And you'll become him?"

"I'm...versatile."

Did he have any idea how intimidating he sounded? He'd never work for what she had in mind. His gravelly voice matched his gravelly demeanor. She needed someone with a softer touch, someone who could attract women of all ages, while providing a buffer between her and certain male clients. The man she hired would need to put paid to any question about her availability on a personal level—without losing potential contributors. Unfortunately, although Shayde could intimidate the hell out of her clients, she doubted she'd retain their business after their first run-in with him.

"I'm sure you're very versatile," she lied smoothly. "But—"

He interrupted without hesitation. "Let's cut through the bull, Mrs. Lonigan. You have a specific type of man in mind that you intend to hire. And you have a specific reason for choosing that type. A reason, I suspect, that you'd prefer to keep to yourself."

The accuracy of his guesses stopped her cold. "How can you possibly know that?"

"One of the assets you may find of particular use is that I have a knack for reading people. An instinct. I see beneath the surface." He eyed her with uncomfortable intensity. "Would you like me to tell you what I've figured out about you?"

"Not really." It was probably the most honest response she'd made to date and he acknowledged it with a knowing smile. "Though I doubt my disapproval is enough to stop you."

"You're right. It's not."

She leaned back in her chair and crossed her legs, striving to give the appearance of a woman at her ease. "Please." She gestured expansively. "Tell me what you see."

His gaze flicked across her hair and it took everything she possessed to keep from shoving the red-gold waves away from her face. Next he took in her almost nonexistent use of makeup before drifting down the length of her body visible from behind the desk. "People consider you open and friendly."

"That's because I am."

He shook his head. "Not even a little. You wear your hair loose so people won't suspect your need for control or how rigidly you apply that control to yourself."

"It's called self-discipline, not control."

"Bull. You like being in control of a situation as much as I do. You're a beautiful woman. Really beautiful. But you're careful not to draw too much attention to that beauty in case it intimidates your clients and co-workers, particularly the men."

"I am *not* intimidating."

"Your remoteness is intimidating. Your innate intelligence and ability is even more so. But you only hit people with those qualities when you're desperate to hold them at a distance."

"You're dead wrong."

He continued as though he hadn't even heard her. "You dress with casual elegance."

"I can't wait to hear why I do that," she muttered.

His mouth curved into a smile that held far too much appeal. "Because you *are* casually elegant. It's not studied or something you've worked to achieve. It's a natural part of you."

A faint flush warmed her cheeks and she silently cursed her pale skin. "Is that it? Are you finished?"

"Not at all. So far everything I've mentioned is surface clutter." He paused and her tension grew as she waited for him to continue. The darkness closed in around them, the night turning dangerous. His voice lowered. "You, Mrs. Lonigan, are a keeper of secrets."

She started in alarm. "Secrets?" He couldn't possibly know that. "What are you talking about?"

"Here—" he swept his hand to indicate her office "—you decorate your surroundings in cheerful, relaxing—bland—colors. But I'm willing to bet that in the privacy of your home you cut loose."

Tess relaxed ever so slightly. "So?"

"I'm guessing that the room you retreat to, your inner sanctum, is filled with bold, striking tones."

She shrugged, unwilling to concede even that much. "Finished?"

"Not even a little. With the exception of a few close friends, no one is allowed too close."

He'd slipped over the line, trespassing on parts of her life he had no business touching. "That's enough."

Apparently he didn't think it was anywhere near enough since he continued as though she hadn't said a word. "You've also been hurt. Badly. And you don't intend to be hurt like that ever again. That's why you need to hire a lover. An employee can be held at a distance. An employee is safe."

How did she make him stop? She didn't want to hear more, but other than physically ejecting him from her office, she couldn't think of a way to end their confrontation. Her hand clenched around her pen. "It would seem that some employees are safer than others." She paused for a moment, then added pointedly, "Oh, that's right. You're not my employee, are you? At this rate, you're not likely to be, either."

He ignored the warning implicit in her comment. "You claim I'm wrong for the job because I'm not like Robert. But that's a lie. You want a lover as different from him as possible."

The pen snapped between her fingers, splattering across her blotter in rivulets as black as the night. Gasping in dismay, she jumped back to escape disaster. With a few shocking words Shayde had succeeded in making her lose her composure. That had never happened before. Avoiding his gaze, she carefully peeled off the ruined sheets of paper covering the felt blotter and dumped them in the trash. The mundane task gave her the few minutes she needed to recover her equilibrium. Somewhat more calm, she returned her attention to Shayde.

"I want you to leave now."

He didn't even shift his position. "Despite what you said earlier, hiring someone like Robert wouldn't work.

And I'll tell you why. You're afraid you'll fall in love with any man who's too much like your late husband and you'll get hurt all over again when he leaves.''

This time he succeeded in provoking a reaction. She planted her palms on her desktop and fought to keep her fury under control. ''That's not a problem since you're not in the least like Robert.''

''I don't doubt that for a minute. I should be the perfect choice since I'm so unlike your late husband. Except for one small detail....''

''Oh, please.'' She held up her hands in surrender. ''Don't keep me in suspense.''

''You also can't hire anyone who attracts you.'' His gaze impaled her. ''And I do attract you, don't I?''

The angry warmth heating her cheeks faded, leaving behind a cold paleness that not only iced her skin, but seeped deep into bones. She pressed her spine tight against the back of her chair. How could he know so much about her? ''Who are you?'' she demanded. ''What do you want from me?''

''I'm the man you're going to hire.''

''Not a chance.''

''Why? Because I see too much?''

She didn't dare admit any such thing. If she did he'd know how accurate his assessment had been. For a brief instant she considered ripping him to shreds with every harsh word she could summon. She was dying to make it crystal clear how mistaken he was in his assessment of her. She didn't find him the least attractive, nor did she have set qualifications for the man she chose other than he be right for the job. Robert had nothing to do with whom she'd choose.

But she didn't dare say any of those things for fear of his seeing through her lies.

She fought for some element of truth with which to argue. "I told you why I won't hire you for the job. You're too rough. Too hard. I need a man who can charm clients, not scare them off." She utilized a hint of the intimidating attitude he'd described earlier. "Let me ask you a question, Shayde. What makes you think you're right for this position?"

"People will believe we're a couple, even though you have doubts," he answered readily enough. "They'll accept it without a single question or any hesitation whatsoever."

"Because you think I'm attracted to you?"

"Because I know you are." He waited for that to sink in before leaning closer. "Now I have a question for you."

"It's not your place to ask questions," she retorted, "only answer them."

He ignored her. "What are you afraid of?"

Her breath quickened and she gazed at him, stunned. Thrusting back her chair, she escaped from the power of those odd eyes. She didn't bother offering a denial. "Thank you, Mr...." She shrugged irritably. "Shayde. Your services won't be required, after all."

"Do you need protection?" he asked softly.

"Didn't you hear me? You can leave now."

"Is there something else you haven't told me? Some*one* else that has you running scared? Or is it just me?"

She wasn't running scared. She was simply at the end of her rope and a wee bit desperate, not that she intended to explain that to him. "I'm not afraid of anything, certainly not of you or any foolish attraction you might think I feel for you. Now, I've asked you to leave politely. Do I have to call security to get rid of you?"

Still he didn't move. "I have the impression you need a strong man and I'm the strongest you're going to find. I suggest you give me a chance." Then he said the unforgivable. "Listen to me, Tess. As long as I'm with you, no one will dare lay a hand on you. You'll be safe, I promise."

He'd slipped beneath her guard again, catching her at her most vulnerable. She fought to hide her distress as she silently shook her head. She wanted to say something…anything. But the words wouldn't come.

"I can protect you."

She almost came undone at the whispered words. No one had ever offered to protect her before. Not her father. Not even Robert. She didn't know how she managed to reply, not that she had any choice if she wanted to get rid of him. "Send me a copy of your résumé," she said in a strangled voice, "and I'll be in touch if I'm interested in your services."

The offer of compromise seemed to work. "Very well. Jeanne has my number if you decide to call." Finally, *finally*, he stood and moved to the door of her office. Once there he turned. "You have one short week to find a man who can play the part of your lover—a lover people will accept without question. And you do need people to believe without question, don't you?"

Damn him! If only he'd stop staring at her with those peculiar silvery eyes, staring as though he knew her every thought before she did. "Yes," she confessed. "I need people to believe without question."

"In that case, you're only going to have one shot at choosing this man. One shot at selling him to your clients and co-workers." Compassion vied with an implacable determination. "Choose wrong and you'll lose everything."

26   THE PROVOCATIVE PROPOSAL

He left the room, closing the door quietly behind him and Tess sank into her chair, thoroughly shaken. It took her a long time before she could bring herself to face the unpalatable truth. She did only have one shot at this. And if she chose wrong, she did stand to lose everything. But the most distressing part of all this was... How did Shayde know that?

CHAPTER TWO

SHAYDE flipped open his cell phone and stabbed in a series of numbers. "Shadoe? It's me."

"Status?" his brother responded.

"Mrs. Lonigan didn't like me," he admitted. "Go figure."

"Were you hired for the job?"

There were times when his older brother could be a major pain. It looked like this would be one of them. "I said she didn't like me." He heard Shadoe's muffled laughter in the background and gritted his teeth. "That generally means, no, I didn't get the job."

"You better fix it. The boss lady won't be happy."

Boss lady? More like dragon lady. Without a doubt, his brother's employer had to be the most exasperating woman Shayde had ever dealt with. Although they'd never met in person because of her almost fanatical determination to protect her identity, he'd discovered during their infrequent phone conversations that she couldn't be charmed and didn't respond to either anger or humor. Once she became fixated on an idea or issue, there she stayed until everyone had given up arguing and fallen in line with her plans, usually out of sheer exhaustion. Only rarely had he been successful winning her over using his own preferred ploy—obstinate, point-by-infuriating-point, just-the-facts-ma'am logic. For a take-charge type of man accustomed to getting his own way, it didn't make for the easiest of relationships.

"Correct the situation?" he demanded. "How am I

supposed to do that? Force her to hire me? That'll go over well."

There was a brief pause before Shadoe said, "Your usual methods will suffice."

"And what methods are those?"

"Bumbling mayhem?"

The muscles in Shayde's jaw clenched. "Yuck it up big brother and I may dump this one in your lap. I'm a volunteer, remember? I don't get paid to screw with people's lives. I do it out of sheer perverse pleasure. Push me and Mrs. Lonigan goes matchless."

Now that he thought about it, he actually liked the sound of that.

"You're to find a weakness to use as leverage," Shadoe retorted. A quick series of computer tones sounded in the background. "I'm sending you an E-mail with a more in-depth report on Mrs. Lonigan than the one you currently have. Use the information you find there. I'll expect another progress report within forty-eight hours."

"I won't blackmail her," Shayde warned. "I made it clear when you approached me about helping out. I don't operate that way."

"The word used was leverage, not blackmail."

"That's a mighty fine line you're drawing there."

There was a pointed silence and then Shadoe's voice rumbled across the line. "Are you refusing the job?"

"Hell, no." But he wanted to. They were making a mistake with this whole ridiculous setup. A bad one. He didn't give a damn if they matched Tess with a dozen eligible men. He didn't have a single doubt that their choice would ultimately prove wrong for her. "Are you certain about this one, bro? Really certain?"

"What do you mean?"

How could he explain gut instinct? He'd lived by it, trusted it, depended on it. And his gut was telling him that Tess Lonigan wouldn't appreciate the Committee's interference in her life. He'd never met a woman quite like her before. He couldn't help remembering how she'd looked when he'd gotten too close—startled, wary, fragile. *Vulnerable.* And yet there had been a steely determination that had overridden her apprehension. While her pansy-blue eyes had revealed her skittishness, she'd faced him with a passionate defiance that had set fire to the night. Nervousness caught within a determined resistance. Fire wrapped in ice. It had made for an intriguing contrast.

Perhaps that explained why he'd pushed so hard. He'd wanted to see the woman behind the mask. He wanted to know her true essence, not the select elements with which she confronted the world around her. And he had seen her, far more than she felt comfortable revealing. He'd also come away from the encounter having formed two ironclad conclusions.

First, this wasn't a woman who would accept help easily or appreciate the deception the Committee was practicing. When she found out the truth, there'd be hell to pay. Second, there was more going on than a mere job promotion, otherwise she wouldn't have taken such an extreme step as hiring a pretend lover. Whatever it was had thoroughly disconcerted the overly controlled Mrs. Lonigan. Which—now that he thought about it— led him to a third conclusion.

She needed him.

"Shayde?" Shadoe's boss joined the conversation. As always her tinny voice sounded odd, almost mechanical. "Explain your reluctance in accepting this assignment."

He released his breath in a sigh. She wouldn't buy

"gut instinct" which meant he better come up with an angle she would buy. Unfortunately, he hadn't found one. Yet. "Tess doesn't strike me as a woman who has much use for a man." Except for him. "Sure, maybe to help out her career. But there's something about her—"

"That's not your decision to make," Shadoe informed him.

Shayde frowned. How did he make his brother understand? "I've met her. You haven't. I have the distinct impression that she's not ready for a relationship."

"We've found the perfect match."

Shayde grimaced. He'd never heard his brother more adamant. "Yeah, great. What if she doesn't want any match, perfect or otherwise?"

It was the boss lady's turn to attack. "The decision has been made. As the Instigator, your job is to initiate the events, not debate the pros and cons. You're to put all the elements in place and allow them to interact."

"And if nothing happens?"

"As always, the ultimate choice remains hers."

"Says you."

"The Committee has never been wrong," she reminded him.

"There's a first time for everything," he retorted. He might as well have saved his breath.

As usual, the two ignored what they didn't want to hear. They made a great team. "Step one is to get the job," Shadoe ordered. "Call us when you've achieved your first objective."

"Yes, sir." Shayde set his jaw. Fine. He'd do his damn job and to hell with his gut instincts. They'd claimed the Cupid Committee had never been wrong. If he couldn't help thinking he'd like to be there when they fell flat on their collective faces, he'd be smart to keep such an aberrant thought to himself. "By tomorrow Mrs. Lonigan and I will be playing the part of lovers."

Shadoe reacted just as he'd anticipated. "Mrs. Lonigan isn't for you, little brother," came the sharp warning.

Shayde didn't bother replying, but snapped the phone closed. Maybe that was so he wouldn't reveal his second aberrant thought.

The hell she isn't.

"Well?" Shadoe asked.

"Interesting development."

He leaned all the way back in his chair and lifted his boot-clad feet to his desktop. "Give him time, boss lady. He's new at this. He'll get it right in the end."

"You should have handled the assignment."

"Nah." Amusement glittered in his eyes like gold dust. "It's more fun this way."

"And if Shayde makes a mistake?" She frowned in displeasure. "It could happen, you know."

"Then we'll be there to pick up the pieces."

"Perhaps."

"What's the matter?" he prompted gently. "Are you having second thoughts?"

"One or two." He could tell she made the confession with great reluctance. "Of all the matches we've arranged, this has the greatest potential for failure."

"Because of Shayde?"

She inclined her head. "And because of Tess Lonigan. What if Shayde decides to take matters into his own hands? It would be like him."

"We've never failed before," he reminded. "We're not going to this time."

She actually smiled. "Promise?"

"Shayde will come through in the end. You have my word of honor."

Tess's phone rang and she picked up the receiver, holding it to her ear with an uplifted shoulder. "Altruistics," she said automatically.

"Dearest, how lovely to speak to you again."

The instant Tess heard the friendly tones she carefully returned her pen to the desktop and straightened in her chair. "Mrs. Smith. This is a surprise."

"I don't know why it would be. I'm sure I mentioned that I'd be in touch."

"So you did," Tess replied. "What can I do for you?"

"I've decided that tomorrow's the day."

Oh, dear. Tess released a silent sigh. She'd been dreading this moment for almost five years. That was how long she'd known Adelaide Smith and that's how long the sweetly stubborn woman had been attempting to find Tess a husband. It didn't matter that she didn't want another husband, or that any of the men Adelaide had forced on her had been abysmal failures. At their last meeting, it had become clear that the woman had decided to go from casual matchmaking to something more drastic.

"Mrs. Smith, I really rather you didn't try and instigate anything between me and your son. He's a potential client and it would be a conflict of interest." Not only that, but Tess suspected her boss had selected Adelaide's son as the Impossible she'd have to turn in order to win her promotion.

"I'm afraid you've left me no choice. You need a man in your life and I'm going to make sure you get one. Dick is perfect for you. I don't know why it didn't occur to me to introduce the two of you before this. Maybe because he was so busy making his millions that I didn't think he'd have time to give you the attention you deserve.''

Lovely. Just what she required—a self-centered mercenary. ''Mrs. Smith, you don't understand. You see, I'm up for this big promotion and—''

''And you have to turn an Impossible. Yes, dear, I know.'' Tess's breath caught in sheer disbelief. How the devil had Adelaide found out about that? As though in response to the silent question, she explained, ''I have my sources. I'm also determined to get what I want. In case you hadn't noticed, I don't give up easily.''

No, she didn't. Which made Tess's position all the more awkward. She'd tried everything over the past several years—saying no, saying yes, explaining ad nauseam, demanding, threatening, begging. Nothing had convinced the woman to stop her efforts. If the Smiths weren't at the top of Altruistic's list of Impossibles they most wanted as contributors, Tess would have taken more drastic action. But how did she tell her boss, Al Portman, that this sweet, adorable woman was as ruthless as a shark when it came to her matrimonial efforts?

Tess gave it one more try. ''What if your son isn't interested in marriage? I'm not.''

Adelaide tutted. ''Don't you see how perfect this will be? I can see it now. You and Dick meet, thanks to my generous efforts. You and Dick fall in love. Dick writes you a nice, fat check that gets you your promotion. You and Dick marry. You and Dick give me grandchildren. You quit your job. And then you and Dick give me more grandchildren. Now isn't that the most perfect idea in the world?''

Grandchildren? Quit? *Grandchildren?* No. Oh, no, no,

no. Desperation drove her to commit to the scheme she'd devised—one she'd prayed she wouldn't need to implement. "It would seem your sources have neglected to keep you adequately apprised," she announced with a calm she was far from feeling.

"Apprised of what, dearest?"

"I'm involved in a serious relationship."

There was a moment of absolute silence. "No, my sources hadn't told me."

"Strange." Tess deliberately infused a bewildered note into her voice. "Considering how serious it is, I'm surprised they didn't think to mention it."

"But Dick—"

"I would be delighted to meet your son in order to discuss a contribution, Mrs. Smith. But I've made a commitment to this other man and I'm not the sort of woman who leapfrogs from relationship to relationship. You wouldn't want me for a daughter-in-law if I were, would you?"

"Of course you're not that type," Adelaide maintained stoutly. "But how do I know if this man's good enough for you?"

"Trust me, he's wonderful."

"Oh, I have the perfect idea." The older woman laughed in delight. "Brilliant, in fact. You bring him to the benefit tomorrow night and I'll look him over. If I'm satisfied, then that will be the end of it. A woman can tell, you know. I'll even talk to Dick about considering your company for a donation. How would that be?"

Tess closed her eyes. What in the world *could* she say? "That would be wonderful, Mrs. Smith. Thank you."

Hanging up the phone, she stared at it for an endless moment. She'd wasted enough time. From the broad hints Al had dropped, he planned to assign Dick Smith as the Impossible who'd make or break her chances at a promotion. Having experienced Adelaide's aggressive tactics firsthand, Tess could kiss that promotion goodbye if she didn't find a way to put an end to any matchmaking attempts before they ever got started.

Tess sighed. Which meant she needed to hire a "significant other" before tomorrow evening. So far she hadn't found anyone more qualified than Shayde, and she doubted that would change within the next twenty-four hours. To be honest, she could look for months and not find anyone to equal him.

Unfortunately, none of the other candidates she'd interviewed had come close to matching either his business qualifications or imposing personal characteristics. Only one thing had kept her from calling Jeanne and instructing her to hire him for the job. Pride. Her breath escaped in a silent sigh. She seemed to have a surfeit of that less-than laudable trait.

Taking a seat at her desk, she punched in Jeanne's number. She didn't bother looking it up. She'd dialed it so many times in the past week she knew it by heart. It only took a moment to confirm her final choice and obtain the necessary information to get in touch with Shayde. She immediately placed the call before she could lose her nerve.

"It's Tess Lonigan," she announced the instant he answered.

"Yes, Mrs. Lonigan." His voice rumbled across the phone lines, the sound every bit as disturbing as when they'd first met. This time she also found it reassuring. How odd. "What can I do for you?"

As if he didn't know. "I've made a final decision

about the job. If you're still available, I'd like to hire you.''

"I'm available," he confirmed. "But I have a few terms we'll need to discuss before I can start working for you.''

She hadn't expected that. "What terms?''

There was a brief pause, and then he said, "I suggest we go over everything in person. Are you free tonight?''

This didn't sound good. She hesitated, debating how best to deal with the situation. As much as she hated to admit it, he had the upper hand. She could argue all she wanted about whatever these terms were, but she'd already committed both of them to attending the benefit. If Shayde decided to force the issue she'd have no choice but to surrender to whatever demands he'd come up with.

Her grip tightened on the receiver. "Yes, I'm free," she admitted shortly. "Where would you like to meet?''

"Your place.''

"No.'' Not a chance in hell.

"Your place," he repeated. "Look, Mrs. Lonigan, Jeanne has had me thoroughly investigated. I'm as safe as you're going to get.''

"Somehow I doubt that," she muttered.

"You had to know this would get personal. You plan to hire a man to act the part of your lover. Did you think the two of you would meet at some central location before attending the various functions you have scheduled? That's not going to work.''

"I—'' She didn't know what she thought. "I guess not.''

"I'll be at your place at eight.'' Voices murmured in the background and he added, "I have to go.''

"Don't you want my address?" she asked dryly.

There was a brief pause and then his husky laugh sounded in her ear, teasing her senses in ways that shocked her. "That might be a good idea."

In only took her a second to relay the information. He hung up immediately afterward and she sat at her desk using every argument at her command to rationalize what she'd just done. Logic didn't work, nor did emotion. Desperation came closest to justifying her actions, but that made her feel worse rather than better. What if she'd hired a lunatic, or some sort of smooth-talking predator? The instant she realized her panic outweighed every other thought or feeling, she snatched up the phone and called her brother. Seth owned a construction company and had access to the precise tool she required to deal with this evening's events.

"Come on, Seth," she pleaded. "You must know someone who can help. I need a big, strong male body in my house while I meet with this guy. And remember, whomever you choose has to be really big and really intimidating, okay? Nothing less than that will work."

Seth didn't cut her any slack. "You're an idiot, Tess. I can't believe someone as smart as you would invite a complete stranger to your house."

"Well, I have. And it still might work, despite what you think. Just have your man at my place before eight. Got it?"

"He'll be there."

"One other question and then I'll let you go."

"Hit me."

"How is the Committee coming along with my request?"

"You're not our only client, Tess. We'll get to Emma and Raine as soon as possible. Besides, I'm willing to bet you'll know how successful we've been before we do. Won't they call you when we dump a pair of perfect matches in their laps?''

''Perfect, huh?''

''Hey, we're good at what we do.''

''You'd better be. Emma and Raine deserve to be happy.''

''They won't just be happy. We guarantee happily-ever-after. Now try and be patient, Tess.''

''I'll be patient if you'll send me a man of my own,'' she teased. ''Only I want mine to be big, bad and as intimidating as they come.''

''No problem. I have the perfect candidate. I'll send him over tonight. Promise.''

Satisfied that she'd protected herself as best she could, she spent the next half dozen hours counting the minutes until her appointment. The time crept by. It didn't help that her workload was unusually slack that day, or that the memories of her initial meeting with Shayde continued to haunt her. His essence permeated her office, whispering to her in a gravelly voice that succeeded in breaking her concentration. At five that evening she escaped Altruistics, though she soon discovered that the wait at home was even worse. After making certain the house would pass muster, she couldn't find anything to hold her attention other than deciding what to wear.

The fact that she'd be consumed with such a trivial issue annoyed her no end. Deliberately, she settled on a comfortable pair of jeans and a sleeveless knit top that left an intriguing inch of torso peeking out between the hem of her top and the waistband of her jeans. Running a comb through her hair, she regarded her image with a trace of defiance. Let him try and call her casually elegant now.

At quarter of eight the doorbell rang and she opened

it to find a huge behemoth of a man taking up the full height and width of her doorway. "Seth sent me," he all but grunted.

He clutched a square of pasteboard in his pawlike fist that turned out to be her brother's business card. On the back, in Seth's handwriting, was scrawled, "Meet Bull. Caution! Feed at your own risk. Keep fingers away from mouth. Operate with care using simple instructions."

Oh, dear. This wasn't quite what she had in mind. She glanced uncertainly at her "protector" before retreating a pace with notable reluctance. "Come in…er…Bull. Can I get you something to drink?"

He shook his head, his bald crown missing the hallway light above him by a scant inch. "Can't. Your brother said no alcohol."

"Oh. I…I meant a soft drink."

His mug crumpled into an expression she took for distaste. "Nah." He folded his massive arms across his equally massive chest and the threads holding his T-shirt together groaned in protest. He regarded her with single-minded intentness. "This guy I'm supposed to protect you from. He threatening you or something?"

"No, no," she hastened to reassure. "I don't know him very well and preferred having someone here until I was sure it was safe."

"You want I should bust 'em if he gives you any bullsh—"

"*No!*" Where had her brother found this guy? She pitched her voice to a soothing level. Poor Shayde. If she didn't do something to protect him, she'd lose both a potential employee, as well as any shot at the job promotion. Maybe a few ground rules were called for. "Just look intimidating, Bull. No hitting. No violence. No physical contact of any sort. Got it?"

His face rumpled up again into what she was fast coming to realize was his unique way of indicating disapproval. "Yeah, okay. Whatever."

"I don't think this will take long. We only have a few matters to discuss. Once we're through, you both can go." Maybe subtlety wasn't the best choice to use with Bull. Maybe big words and long sentences weren't, either. "Stay here until he goes. I want you both to leave together. Got it?"

His irritated shrug didn't strike her as an agreement. But that might have something to do with the fact that she hadn't fully learned Bull-speak, yet. For all she knew a shrug might mean, "Yes, ma'am, whatever you say, ma'am." Then again, it could also mean, "I don't take orders from anyone, I simply pound iron spikes into cement with my bald little head and I do it whenever the spirit moves me."

If the doorbell hadn't rung, she'd have gone over the instructions once more in single syllable words to make certain Bull understood them. That way she'd have done her best to convey her intent, even if he chose not to follow her directions. Instead, she shot him a warning look—like that would do any good—and hastened to the door.

Shayde stood on her porch.

"Please, come in," she invited with a cool formality she was far from feeling. Standing to one side, she allowed him across the threshold.

Bull lumbered into view and Shayde slowly closed the door. Glancing at Tess, he lifted an eyebrow. "A friend of yours?"

"We just met."

Shayde inclined his head in her bodyguard's direction. "Bull. How's it going?"

Bull's face broke apart in a huge grin. "Heyya, Shayde. What the hell are you doin' here?"

"I have an appointment with Mrs. Lonigan."

"'Pointment?" A deep frown furrowed his massive brow and his brain cells shifted into high gear. One cell after another ignited until a full half dozen erupted into a sputtering flame. Then he turned on Tess his face collapsing into an expression of deep affront. "*This* is the guy I'm supposed to bust up for you?"

She started in alarm. "*No!* That's not what I—"

Shayde folded his arms across his chest and shook his head in mock reproof. "Not an auspicious start to our relationship, Mrs. Lonigan."

"I didn't ask him to—" she attempted to protest.

"Sorry, Miz Lonigan. But I can't take on Shayde," Bull interrupted. He ticked off on a beefy finger. "First, I'd get in trouble with everybody if I tried."

That caught her attention. "Everybody? Who's everybody?"

"Your brother, his brother, and—" He shot an apprehensive glance in Shayde's direction. "I mean... I mean... You know. *Everybody.*"

"Good save, Bull," Shayde murmured in an encouraging aside.

The huge man plowed determinedly onward. "And second, I'd lose the fight."

He'd momentarily distracted Tess by counting so high. As a result, it took her an instant to assimilate what he'd said. "You'd lose?" She didn't bother to conceal her astonishment. "*You,* Bull?"

He couldn't seem to decide whether to preen or take offense. "I'm the best," he muttered, squirming like a schoolboy. "But Shayde's better."

"I can take it from here, old friend," Shayde inserted.

Bull jerked to attention. "Right. No need for me to hang around. I'll push off then."

"Wait a minute," Tess objected. "You were supposed to stay until we were through."

"Oh, no, Miz Lonigan. You just wanted me to stay to make sure you was safe," Bull explained earnestly. "I know you might find this hard to believe, but you'll be safest with Shayde. Safer even than with me."

"An honest assessment of the situation," Shayde approved.

Before she could voice a single word of protest, Bull opened the front door and maneuvered his bulk through it before slamming it shut behind him. The windows closest to the door rattled so hard it was a wonder they didn't shatter. She stared after him in disgust. "This isn't going at all the way I'd planned."

"Nervous about our meeting?"

His voice sounded even more like ground glass than normal and abraded every bit as much. She spun away from the door to face him. "Since I don't know you, I thought I'd play it smart."

"Do you invite Bull over for every first date?"

"All of them," she lied. "If they pass his inspection and don't run screaming into the night, there's a second date."

He didn't bother to remind her that not two minutes ago she'd claimed she'd just met Bull. Instead, he smiled and she felt the warmth melt deep into her bones. "Since I haven't run out on you, I guess there's hope for us."

She'd been a fool to think Shayde could possibly be either a lunatic or a smooth-talking predator. This man didn't use deceit to achieve his ends. He didn't need to. All he had to do was flash that killer smile of his and he'd get his way every time. All in all, she found her new employee quite impressive. With a gorgeous set of shoulders, a lean muscular physique and eyes that burned with an intensity that threatened to steal her breath, she found it increasingly difficult to remember why he'd come.

Her mouth firmed. Enough already. He'd invited himself here for a reason and if she were smart, she wouldn't waste any time finding out what he wanted before showing him the door. "How do you know Bull?" she asked, hoping the topic would help them regain a business footing.

"We go way back," Shayde answered with irritating vagueness. He glanced around the hallway. "Where's the inner sanctum?"

So much for focusing on business. If he kept diffusing that focus, she'd have a rough time of it this evening. "You won't be going there."

"Afraid it'll confirm my guess?"

She refused to be drawn. "I don't know you well enough to show you my inner anything."

He lifted an eyebrow at her phrasing. "Do you know anyone that well?"

She didn't bother answering, but nodded toward a corridor leading to the rear of the house. "Come on, Shayde. I'll take you as far as the kitchen. We can talk over coffee."

"I'll go as far as you're willing to take me on a first date. Coffee sounds like an excellent start."

She couldn't help smiling. "Fair warning, coffee is the start *and* finish. And the kitchen is as far as you'll be invited."

He shook his head in pretend dismay. "You're a tough first date."

With luck, she'd remain a tough first date, as well as

a tougher second, third and fourth. "I gather your first dates tend to be more interesting?"

"As a rule."

"Sorry to disappoint."

"We'll see how disappointed I am when the evening's over."

Enough small talk. Gesturing for him to follow, she led the way to the kitchen. It only took a moment to start the coffee perking. "When we spoke, you mentioned there'd be terms to discuss before you took the job." She removed a pair of mugs from the cabinet. "What terms?"

"I see you're a woman who prefers to get to the point." He rubbed his hands together. "Okay. Let's get to it."

"Please, do," she encouraged dryly. Anything but stand around and allow all that impressive masculinity to permeate her home. Bad enough that he'd done it to her office.

"You want us to act the part of lovers, right? Here are my conditions." He paused again and she had the unnerving impression that his comments were off-the-cuff rather than planned in advance. "Number one. We spend time together before our first public appearance so we can learn to play our roles convincingly."

"Impossible. The benefit's tomorrow night."

"Then we'd better get busy."

She dismissed his demand with a quick wave of her hand. "It's totally unnecessary, Shayde. If we tell people we're a couple they'll believe it without our having to practice." She used the excuse of pouring coffee to justify turning her back on him. "How do you take it?"

"Black and strong."

"Black I can do. I can't make any promises about the other."

"I'll take my chances. You don't strike me as a weak tea coffeemaker." He waited for her to approach. The instant she set the mugs on the table, he caught hold of her hand. Her reaction was as immediate as it was instinctive. She jerked away from him, taking a hasty step backward. His smile lacked any trace of humor. "Do I need to say, 'I told you so'?"

Damn him. She hated that he was right as much as she hated what she'd have to do to correct the situation. Perhaps his comments weren't as off-the-cuff as she'd thought. "Point taken. We need to become...comfortable with one another."

To her relief he didn't laugh at the understatement. "Second condition. We handle our public performance my way."

She didn't like the sound of that. "It's my career that's at stake," she argued. "I won't give up control of that to a temporary employee."

"You will if you want to work with me." His tone warned the matter wasn't open for negotiation. "Third condition."

"Tell me it's also your last."

"It's also my last condition."

"Not that I'm agreeing to your other ones, you understand," she hastened to insert. She desperately needed to remain in control, though she suspected it would prove no more than a comforting illusion. "I can only promise to take your requests into consideration."

"Understood." His smile appeared more genuine this time. "My third condition is that we move in together."

CHAPTER THREE

SHAYDE couldn't believe he'd said that. But now that he had, he found the idea all too appealing. What had happened to instigating a relationship with the man the Committee had selected for Tess? Somehow it had become lost in a more primitive, more urgent directive.

She took a swift step away from his chair, staring at him with an appealing combination of bewilderment and disbelief. He'd shaken her, finally managing to strip away the professional mask she used to hold people at a safe distance. But he'd also uncovered a vulnerability that slipped beneath his own guard, prompting an unexpected desire to protect her—even from himself.

"Have you lost your mind?" she demanded.

"No."

"Then I must have lost mine thinking we could ever work together. Thank you for coming this evening, Mr...." Irritation flickered in her expressive blue eyes, not that it erased the vulnerability lingering there. "Shayde. But I'll contact Jeanne in the morning and set up an interview with the other person she had in mind for the job."

He knew fear when he saw it. And this lady was definitely running scared. Now why would one outrageous suggestion cause such panic? "Your benefit is tomorrow night. Do you honestly think you'll find someone who can do the job by then?"

"You seem to think you can do it." She shrugged with an awkwardness he'd have sworn she didn't possess. It spoke of an uncomfortable awareness—of him, of the solitude created by time and place, of the ramifications of his request. But most of all it spoke of a need that simmered beneath the surface. Perhaps another man wouldn't have picked up on it. Too bad he wasn't just any man, at least not when it came to Tess. "If you can handle the job, Shayde, why not someone else?"

"I'll show you."

He ignored the voice inside his head, the one bellowing orders he had no interest in acknowledging, let alone obeying. They were smart, common sense orders, he had to admit. Orders like… Leave the house. Leave the room. Leave Tess untouched. She's not for you. Too bad common sense chose that moment to desert him. Standing, he knocked his chair aside and allowed sheer, raw instinct to take over.

Wrapping an arm around her waist, he hauled her close and took her mouth with all the finesse of a lust-crazed caveman. Until that moment he'd have sworn he didn't possess any Neanderthal tactics. Wrong. It would seem he possessed more than his fair share. Perhaps it was a genetic thing, remaining dormant until the right time and right woman. Or perhaps he was just an idiot. Yeah, that seemed more likely.

Especially considering the tactics didn't work.

She didn't melt into his embrace as he'd hoped, but slammed backward against the counter. Her arms and legs pinwheeled until the two of them became entangled in the most awkward position imaginable. Worse, she'd tilted her head the wrong way and their noses squashed together while her lips bunched up on one side of his mouth. He attempted to correct the misalignment. Arms and legs retangled into a ridiculous series of kinks and knots. And now her mouth threatened to slide off his chin while her nose got lost somewhere in the vicinity of his cheek.

Hell. "Sixth grade," he muttered.

Her mouth twitched. *"Mmfpht?"*

He pulled away slightly and eyed her in half amusement, half resignation. "Lisa Penn in the sixth grade. She was the first girl I ever kissed and it was the worst experience of my life. Probably of hers, too."

Tess attempted to unravel some of their body parts without noticeable success. Her elbow found his gut with unerring accuracy and he manfully suppressed a groan. Served him right for grabbing her in the first place. "I don't know how to break this to you, but you haven't improved much since then," she complained.

He cautiously rearranged arms, legs, hands and feet until they could each stand on their own and weren't in imminent danger of injuring anything irreplaceable. "I admit that first attempt didn't go well. Next time—"

"There won't be a next time," she interrupted. "All you've done with that little stunt is convince me that we could never work together."

"What I've proven is that we're going to have one hell of a time convincing people we're a couple—unless we find a way to coordinate our angle of trajectory."

She released her breath in the sort of sigh women use when men act like men. "An interesting way of phrasing it."

"Maybe it's our rate of entry that's screwed up. Or perhaps magnetic interference has sent our gyroscopes into a tailspin." He rubbed a hand across his jaw. "Whatever's causing the problem, we're definitely off on our docking procedure."

"I am *not* some sort of space station and you're not

the astronaut assigned to board her...it..." She glared in frustration. *"Me!"*

She was right, not that he'd admit such a thing. At some point his primary job had fallen by the wayside. Logic, discretion, even basic intellect had gotten lost beneath a far stronger imperative. "That's where you're wrong. Perhaps I could have chosen a better analogy, but the bottom line is you need someone you can respond to on a physical, as well as an intellectual level. I'm that man."

"No, you're not. It only took one kiss to confirm that."

His jaw assumed a stubborn set. "That kiss didn't prove anything other than I caught you by surprise and you weren't willing to let down your guard long enough to follow your natural urges."

"There's a reason for that."

"Fear?"

"No! You're my employee, not my lover."

"You hired me to be both," he couldn't resist pointing out.

She didn't let him get away with it. "I hired you to *be* my employee and to *play* the part of my lover. That doesn't mean you're supposed to grab and kiss your boss. Or is that standard operating procedure with you?"

"I believe you're the first employer I've ever grabbed and kissed." He eyed her with amused frankness. "To be honest, I'm giving that approach a serious rethink. I'm not convinced it's a total success."

"It's not even a little success. All it's going to do is get you fired."

He lifted an eyebrow in question. "Are you firing me?"

She wanted to, he could tell. At a guess the thought

of suffering through another round of interviews saved him from complete disaster. "I'm willing to let it go this once." A hint of steel threaded her voice. "But I won't agree to your terms."

That's what she thought. "You're not willing to spend time with me before the benefit?" he asked mildly.

She spun away, refusing to face him until she'd put as much distance between them as possible. "When do you suggest we spend that time? The benefit's tomorrow night. It can't be tomorrow during the day. I have a job. Am I supposed to neglect it just so we can become better acquainted? Not a chance."

He pointed out the obvious. "There's tonight. Are you willing to work on our relationship now?"

She gave it serious thought. "I guess."

Her unenthusiastic response was the best he could hope for. He didn't bother pushing for more. "Then that's the first condition met. Talk to me about your problems with my second condition. What's wrong with taking my recommendations for how we interact in public?"

"I can't allow you to jeopardize my career."

"I'm not talking about jeopardizing your career. I'm talking about how we sell ourselves as a couple. If I take your hand in mine while we're sitting at the dinner table, I expect you to follow my lead and not jerk free at the first opportunity."

"We weren't in public when I did that," she retorted, stung. "I wasn't expecting you to touch me."

"I may catch you by surprise when we're with your employer or a client. What are you going to say then? 'Sorry about that. We didn't practice being lovers long enough, but hang on. We'll get it right this next time around.'"

"Don't be ridiculous."

"You've got it. I am being ridiculous. You won't need to say a word because our awkwardness with each other will be obvious to even the most casual bystander. Look at that damned kiss. We can't even manage something that simple."

He'd hit a sore point and in response she snarled herself into a knot again—arms folded across her chest, knees locked together at an awkward angle, mouth compressed into a line that would have done a schoolmarm proud. "Since we won't be kissing in public or in private or anywhere in between, it won't be a problem."

"Oh, it's going to be a problem," he warned softly.

"Let me guess. In order to—how did you phrase it?" She unsnarled long enough to rescue her coffee mug as she considered her choice of words. "Oh, right. In order to perfect our docking procedure, you want us to live together?"

He tried not to wince. "It would help. There's nothing like sharing pajamas to take the formality out of a relationship."

"Let me guess. The catch is that you don't wear pajamas."

He didn't say a word. He didn't have to.

She retreated into formality. "You don't seem to understand that this job won't last more than a couple of days. You'll only be around my co-workers and clients for a few brief hours, at most. We can fake a relationship for that long without turning it into a major production."

"It will only take you a day or two to turn an Impossible?"

"If I'm lucky."

"What if you aren't?" He waited for that to impact before adding, "And what about afterward? Let's say you get the promotion. Won't you need us to continue to maintain a pretense for a while? Or will this mysterious problem you're having—the one that convinced you to hire me in the first place—disappear the minute you win your promotion?''

"Why are you doing this?" He found it telling that she deliberately avoided answering his question. Even more telling, she wrapped her hands around the coffee mug and retreated behind a facade of calm he knew she was far from feeling. "I'm hiring you for a simple job and for some reason you're pushing this far beyond the scope of your employment. Why?"

Hell. He'd overplayed his hand. "I take my job seriously."

She immediately rejected that one. "It's more than that. How do you know Bull? I know him through my brother. What about you?"

He made a split-second decision. "I know him through Seth, too."

Tess's hand jerked and coffee sploshed over the rim. Clearly, he'd shocked her with his admission. "You know—"

"Seth. Yes. We were at university together."

"You never said. *He* never—" She shook her head. "I don't understand any of this."

Time for a little honesty. "After you hired me, you phoned your brother for a..." He leaned against the counter across from her, choosing his words with care. "I guess you'd call it a protector, for want of a better word. Let's just say Bull wasn't Seth's first choice."

"He got in touch with you?" she asked incredulously.

"Seth didn't realize I was the immediate cause of your problem and since I'm the best man for the job, he called me." A quick grin slashed across his face. "Face it, even Bull admits I'm the best."

Her eyes narrowed. "Really? Then what are you doing working for me as a paid escort?"

Shayde lifted his shoulder in a casual shrug. "I'm between jobs."

Fortunately, she didn't follow up on that one, instead seizing on a different and more immediate concern. "What did you tell Seth? About us, I mean."

He debated for a brief second. "I told him you needed an escort for business functions." Was she concerned about how her brother might react? "I had the impression he thought it was a practical decision based on your current situation."

A hint of relief brightened her eyes. "Why didn't he simply vouch for you? Why send Bull?"

"He figured you might not take his word for it, that you'd think he was blowing you off with excuses. So he sent someone who'd convince you I was safe."

A genuine smile eased her mouth. Heaven help him, but she was beautiful. Did she have any idea the effect of that smile on a man? "Bull did convince me you'd make a good protector," she conceded. "But I'm not sure how safe I'd consider either of you."

"There's a reason for that."

"Which is?"

"I make an excellent protector against outsiders." He fixed her with a look that warned that the caveman hadn't been fully contained. "But not necessarily from myself."

"Then I'll stay on my guard." She took a sip of coffee and locked gazes with him over the rim. Her expression warned that she'd fight him every inch of the way. "Which brings us back to your terms."

"So we're in agreement. You accept all my conditions." He managed to make the statement with a straight face. Barely.

"On your first two conditions, yes. But you're not moving in here. I don't care how many people vouch for you."

He didn't care about the third one. He couldn't even say why he'd thrown it in, other than to see what it would take to slip beneath her guard and prompt a response. He'd gotten what he really wanted with the other two points "Fine. Then we start now."

She backed into an angle formed by the kitchen counters, her hold on the mug turning into a white-knuckled grip. "Now?"

Did she have any idea how blatantly she projected her emotions? Somehow he doubted it or she'd have taken steps to disguise them. Communicating her feelings so clearly couldn't help in her dealings with clients. All they had to do was look at her to know her every thought.

Or perhaps her behavior was unique to this situation, a singular response to him as a man. If so, she'd be wise to hide her reaction. Observing her standing there, wary and defenseless, stirred something fiercely masculine within him, an irresistible urge to give chase in direct opposition to her nervous retreat. It was man versus woman at its most primitive, perfuming the air with the hungry scent of want. He found himself obeying the ancient call without thought.

He shoved off from the counter and approached. "You promised we'd spend time together tonight." He stopped a scant foot away, noting that her breathing had kicked up several notches. "I suggest we get started."

"I have a better suggestion," she hastened to propose.

"We can take a few minutes before the benefit to become better acquainted. Say...an hour to gain a working familiarity right before the evening begins. "

"We could do it that way...." He snagged a rosy curl, allowing the strand to wrap possessively around his finger. "If you were the one in charge. But you're not."

"We had this discussion, remember?" she tried again. "I'm your employer."

"You pay my salary, but I make the decisions." He tugged her closer. "Or did you plan to violate the terms of our agreement so soon?"

"No. Yes." She glared at him in frustration. "You're making this very difficult."

He offered a sympathetic smile. "I have a reputation for that. Let's see if I can't make it a little easier for you."

Rescuing her coffee cup before she dropped it, he set it on the counter. Then he slid his fingers into her hair and tipped her face up to his. "What are you doing?" she demanded.

"Correcting a mistake."

"We agreed that there wouldn't be any more kissing."

He smiled at the disgruntled complaint. "That was before you promised to do things my way."

A hint of color clung to her cheekbones and a distressing defenselessness swept across her face. "You said you'd make this easier. I think I should warn you that this doesn't feel particularly easy."

"Give it a chance. We only have twenty-four hours to become accustomed to each other's touch. That's a lot of ground to cover in very little time."

"I'd rather become accustomed without touching."

He didn't doubt that for a minute. "Sorry. It has to

be my way. But you won't suffer for long." He lowered his head and murmured against her lips, "Trust me."

He didn't give her a chance to think, let alone protest. This time he managed a successful docking and fully covered her mouth. He even managed to align their noses properly. Falling into the kiss, he submersed himself in the taste and feel of her. Everything about her felt incredible. Her hair. Her lips. Her skin. And everything about her aroused him, desire igniting a flame that could build into something far more intense with very little effort.

At first, she stood rigid within his grasp, not fighting, but not participating, either. "Relax," he encouraged. "We're not going to do anything that makes you uncomfortable. You set the pace."

Her hands slid up to his shoulders, holding on lightly as though she couldn't decide whether to slide into the embrace or push him away. "You feel...different."

"Different, how?"

"Hard." She didn't say it coyly, as some women would. She was being serious, not playing sexual word games. "Uncompromising."

"I'm both of those things," he admitted without apology. "But I don't use those qualities to hurt people."

"Even in your role as protector?"

"No way. Not against the good guys."

That caught her attention. "Am I one of the good guys?"

Did she doubt it? "Absolutely."

He tried their kiss again, using more caution this time, setting a slower pace. Her hands slipped upward, smoothing across his shoulders in a light, experimental touch. And though she relaxed into him somewhat, it wasn't a total surrender to the embrace. Her lips softened, but didn't part. Her breathing quickened, but didn't grow urgent. And yet, he could feel her building passion, just as he could feel the desperate control she maintained over it.

He could sense she wanted to let go. So why didn't she follow her instincts and lower her guard enough to free the desire simmering beneath the surface? Why did she resist what they both craved? Forcing the issue hadn't worked. Nor had coaxing.

He eased back and studied her upturned face. "It's a start, I guess."

"Not a very successful one," she admitted wryly.

No. The kiss hadn't been as successful as he'd have liked. They continued to respond like two strangers, their bodies instinctively fighting to find a comfortable fit— and not succeeding. And he could guess why. "It wasn't so bad," he reassured. "Not when you take into consideration that we don't know each other very well. I also suspect you're the sort of woman who prefers to build a relationship the slow, old-fashioned way."

She shrugged. "What's wrong with that?"

"Nothing, except we don't have time for slow and old-fashioned."

She fought free of his hold, "Don't you get it? I don't want a relationship with you. I don't want a relationship with anyone."

"Yes. I got that." The Committee was having trouble comprehending it. "The question is…since you don't want a relationship, why do you need to fake one? What is it about this job promotion that's forcing you to pretend you're involved with a man?"

"That's not your concern."

"It is when it interferes with the job you've asked me to do." He studied her with a frown, cautiously feeling his way. The hell with it. He'd go with his instincts and if his observations started trouble...well, he was used to that. "You're fiercely independent, a woman who takes charge of her own destiny, someone who strikes me as honest and aboveboard, and yet, you've been forced to create this deception in order to get ahead at work. Why?"

"As I said—"

An unpleasant thought occurred to him. "Is one of your clients pressuring you for sex?"

"No!"

She reacted with such shocked conviction that he didn't doubt she was telling the truth. Still... He was close. He could sense it. "But you're having trouble with a client. And somehow this trouble will be averted if we're perceived as lovers. Why won't you tell me what the problem is? Maybe I can help."

"I don't intend to explain anything to you for the simple fact that I don't—" She stopped abruptly.

He finished her statement. "You don't trust me?" She nodded abruptly and he decided to let her off the hook. "Fair enough. Trust can't be forced, any more than an honest relationship can. But since we have to give the perception of both, I suggest we go back into the hallway."

"Are you leaving?"

"Don't sound so hopeful." Maybe it was just as well Shadoe hadn't chosen him for Tess. He didn't envy the poor fool who tried to get her to the altar. He'd probably have to hog-tie and drag her there, kicking and screaming the entire way. "No, I'm not leaving. I want to try something else. There's not enough room in the kitchen for what I have in mind."

She didn't argue. Shrugging, she led the way. Once

there, she turned to face him. "Now what?" she asked uncertainly.

"Now we dance."

"Dance?" She stared at him as though he'd lost his mind. "There's no music."

"All the better. This way our bodies can hear each other."

She released her breath in a gusty sigh. "Okay. I get it now. You're one of *those* guys."

His brows snapped together. What the devil was she talking about? "What do you mean...*those*," he demanded suspiciously.

She waved her hand through the air. "You know. One of those New Age types. Weird mumbo-jumbo philosophies, crystals, dancing without music. You know. *Those* guys."

Aw, hell. He didn't see a viable way to refute that one. Considering how stubborn she could be, she'd view any form of protest as confirmation of her suspicions, while out-and-out arguing would only serve to cement her position. He didn't like no-win situations. They ticked him off. Wrapping his hands around her jean-clad hips, he yanked her into the cradle of his thighs. Her shocked gasp pleased him no end.

"You got me, babe," he growled. "There's no point in arguing with fact. I have crystals strung from one end of my house to the other. Want a mood adjustment? I've got just the rock to do it." He slid a hand up her spine, locking her close. "And they haven't written a philosophy book that I haven't read and found a doctrine or two to incorporate into my own personal code. Makes it confusing on occasion, but what the hell. At least it covers every eventuality."

It took her two deep breaths before she recovered her

self-possession enough to respond. "Let me guess. I'm not as accurate a judge of character as you."

He rocked his hips in a slow circle, the hand he'd anchored on her hip encouraging her to follow his lead. "Do I look like the sort of man who'd put up with mumbo-jumbo?"

A nervous laugh slipped free. "Did you know that your eyes get all smoky when you're upset?"

To his frustration, her movements ran counter to his. Rather than matching his steps with instinctive ease, she zigged in opposition to his zags. And when she wasn't zigging all over the place, she abused his poor toes by cheerfully stomping all over them. At least, he assumed she was cheerful about it. She sure as hell didn't look apologetic.

"Everyone should have a warning sign," he gritted out. "I'm impressed you've figured out mine so fast. I'll be more impressed if and when you take that warning to heart."

She abused his toes some more before peeking up at him with the sort of sweet, innocent smile that instantly put him on red alert. "You might not have noticed, but this doesn't seem to be working."

"It might work better if you'd stop trying to lead. That's my job."

"Sorry." Not that she looked the least sorry. "I'm used to being the one in charge."

"That makes two of us."

Tess slowed to a halt. "Okay, Shayde. We've danced. Now explain why it was necessary other than to prove that we're as incompatible at this as everything else we've tried."

Did she really not know or was she being deliberately obtuse? "Haven't you ever watched couples dance?"

"Sure."

"Can't you tell the ones who've danced together before from the ones who haven't? The ones who are lovers versus acquaintances?"

A swift shadow slipped across her face. "Yes."

"There's an intimacy to their movements. A knowing. Their bodies are in rhythm with each other." He pulled her close again. "Come on. Let's give it another try."

A hint of strain etched her features. "I'd rather not."

"One dance, Tess," he insisted. "If we can't even manage that much, how are we supposed to play our roles in a convincing manner?"

She fixed her gaze on a point just over his shoulder. "We'll give it one more try and that's it. If it still doesn't work, we give up."

He kept to the most simplistic of dance steps. It didn't seem to help. "Relax, will you?"

"I'm trying!"

"Try harder." She'd managed to wriggle away from him again and he settled a hand in the hollow of her back and realigned their bodies. "Lean into me, Tess. Try and pick up on the cues I'm giving you. Can you feel my thigh and hip, the slight push?"

"I'm feeling too much thigh and hip," she retorted, an unmistakable edge to her voice. "Not to mention far too much push."

He'd never held a woman in his arms who was so resistant and he released his breath in a sigh. "Okay, I get that you don't like having me touch you. Tough luck, sweetheart. You hired me for a job and we're going to get it done one way or another. I suggest you close your eyes and remember all the reasons you hired me. If those reasons are important enough, you'll find a way to make this work. Now stop fighting me and do what I say or give up on your damn promotion.''

Shock held her rigid for a brief instant, then her chin firmed. Slapping a hand on his shoulder, she thrust her hips close to his. "Dance," she ordered through gritted teeth.

"You got it."

He swung her in another easy circle. This time she followed his movements with only a single stumble. Recovering swiftly, she managed to avoid his toes and even succeeded in mating her steps to his. After negotiating a single circuit of the room, he tightened his hold before Tess could escape.

"Again," he insisted.

This time went more easily, a natural fluidity replacing their earlier awkwardness. To his satisfaction, she anticipated his maneuvers and followed with ease. She had a natural rhythm, though he'd never have guessed it based on their first stab at this. Once they'd completed the second circle, she tried to end the dance and he stopped her.

"Once more."

Her mouth tightened, but she didn't protest. He made the dance steps a bit more complicated, not that she had a problem with them. Acknowledging the challenge with a knowing smile, she matched him move for move, fitting her body tightly to his.

He sensed it then. For just an instant she relaxed into him the way lovers were meant to. The music came from within, their rhythms combining, blending, entwining. And he did what came naturally. He gathered her up and made love to her with every sway and spin and step. Her response was all he could have wished. Her heart pounded out the beat of their inner music and he followed it, answering the silent call with the sort of lingering caresses lovers delight in.

She shivered, her body softening against his, and a sensual awareness gathered in her eyes. Moistening her lips, she lifted her chin as though readying for his kiss. Everything about her echoed that readiness—the flush darkening her cheekbones, how she responded to his touch, looked at him, inhaled him. He couldn't resist touching her and her breasts peaked beneath the sweep of his fingertips. If anyone had seen her now, they wouldn't question that Tess was his lover. This was how their kiss should have been, and how she should have reacted each of the times he touched her.

And then it ended almost as soon as it had begun. Twisting free of his hold, she stared at him, appalled. "Have you lost your mind?" She crossed her arms across her chest. "What do you think you're doing?"

"Dancing," he stated succinctly.

"That wasn't dancing. You touched me. It was...was—" She stared at him as though he'd just slimed his way out from beneath a pile of moldy debris. "That should never have happened. How could you!"

Now she'd really ticked him off. "I could. I would. And—here's a newsflash for you, sweetpea—someone should have long ago." He closed the distance between them. "And not only did it happen, but now that I know what it takes to get through to you, I'll make certain it happens on a regular basis. Got it?"

CHAPTER FOUR

TESS shook her head, not backing down an inch. "I'm not going to give you the opportunity to try anything like that again. I forgot myself for a minute while we were dancing, but it was a one time deviation."

Shayde swore beneath his breath. Deviation? She considered what they'd experienced a deviation? What was it about this woman? She had the uncanny knack of burrowing under his skin and provoking an itch he didn't have a hope in hell of scratching. That had never happened before.

"Here's another newsflash for you, Tess. You better start deviating a hell of a lot more often or this whole scheme is going to fail and fail miserably. For just an instant there, you let down your guard. You reacted like a woman's supposed to react when she's in the arms of her lover."

Her mouth formed a stubborn line. "You're not my lover and I don't want to dance like that with you."

"Why?"

She started to answer, then turned her back on him at the last second. "You've proven your point," she announced. "This isn't working. We have trouble walking and talking at the same time, let alone dancing. I suggest we avoid the dance floor at tomorrow's benefit."

"That's not what I'm saying." He fought to control his frustration with only limited success. "You know what I'm trying to accomplish and you're making this

64

more difficult than it needs to be. Why? What the hell's going on, Tess?"

"It's late. You should go now."

"It's not even nine. And we're not finished prepping."

She spun around, facing him once again. Her eyes had darkened to a pain-filled shade of indigo and she compressed her lips, no doubt to prevent them from trembling. A remoteness clung to her, her expression so defensive he suspected that one wrong word would end his job before he'd begun. "Enough, Shayde. I'm not going to dance with you anymore and that's final."

And then it hit him. He lowered his voice to its most soothing pitch. Not that it would sound terribly soothing. He'd never had the type of voice capable of calming hysterical children or mesmerizing rabid dogs. His success came from issuing rough-edged instructions that people were rarely willing to question or challenge. "Our dancing together reminds you of Robert, doesn't it?"

She instantly denied his guess. "Wrong."

Shayde frowned. What could have upset her so badly? If it wasn't something she and her late husband had done before... Aw, hell. Then it was something they hadn't. How could he have been so thoughtless? "You're upset because you and Robert were never in synch dancing. When I was describing how lovers look when they're in each other's arms, how there's an intimacy to their movements—you never experienced that with Robert, did you?"

Her jaw worked for a second before she shook her head. "No."

She spoke the single word so softly he almost didn't catch it. No wonder his words had hurt. That hurt must have been compounded when he and Tess had achieved what she never had with her late husband, even if it had only been for a brief moment. Compassion filled him and he struggled to find a way to repair the damage. "Okay, so you and Robert didn't dance well together. That doesn't invalidate your relationship. You must know that."

"Could we please change the subject?"

"If you don't want to dance at the benefit, we won't. But we're not finished. We still have to be comfortable enough with each other so that people believe we're a couple. Will you work with me a little longer?"

She thrust a hand through her hair, upsetting the neatly brushed waves. The hallway light tangled in the soft curls, highlighting the varying shades of red and gold. Her movement also lifted the hem of her knit top, exposing the creamy expanse of her abdomen. She was a woman of contrasts, an intriguing mixture of flame and ice. As hard as she tried to hold people at a distance, her innate warmth drew them to her, tempting them to risk the bitter cold for a chance to luxuriate in the balmy heat. And all the while, she remained oblivious to her own attraction. Or perhaps she simply didn't want to know, preferring to focus on her career to the exclusion of all else.

"What more is there?" she asked.

"A movie and some popcorn."

Confusion gave her features a heartbreaking vulnerability. "You're asking me out?"

"No. I'm asking you to microwave a bag of popcorn, stick a tape in your VCR and sit with me for the duration of a single movie."

He could tell she wanted to argue. After a full minute

of debate, she nodded in agreement. "One movie and you'll leave?"

"That's it."

"And by the time it's through, people will believe we're lovers?"

He shrugged. "Let's just say we should have a reasonable chance of pulling it off." But only if they were very, very lucky.

There had to be something wrong with his suggestion, but Tess was darned if she could figure out what it might be. It didn't take more than five minutes to discover what she hadn't taken into consideration. The first clue came when he stuck the tape in the VCR and snapped off the lights.

"What are you doing?" she demanded.

"Turning off the lights."

"That's obvious. The question is...why?"

"Because I watch movies in the dark. It sets the mood."

Mood. Uh-oh. After what had happened in the hallway, she wasn't interested in setting a mood, unless it involved a lot of light, a distance of several feet between them and as little conversation as possible. She backed from the room. "Feel free to start without me. I'll get the popcorn."

Heading for the kitchen—Tess refused to admit she was beating a hasty retreat—she decided she'd take as long as possible to pop a bag in the microwave. Unfortunately, that would only use up a scant three minutes. Pushing the appropriate buttons, she leaned against the kitchen counter and glared at the microwave. This wasn't working out the way she'd planned. Not at all.

It wouldn't be so bad if Shayde would simply behave

the way she expected an employee to behave. But he'd kissed her, danced with her. And she'd— She thrust away from the counter and paced from one end of the kitchen to the other. Darn it all! She'd responded to him. Not only had she thoroughly enjoyed his kiss, but she'd practically made love to him in the hallway during that dance. Why had her body chosen that moment to rebel, and with Shayde of all people?

She'd managed to hold men at a comfortable distance for nine long years, to put her career ahead of any sort of personal involvement. After Robert's death, it had been safer, less emotionally devastating. And yet in a few short hours, Shayde had succeeded in breaking through those barriers.

Face it, girl. The painful fact was, she felt torn, a perfectly normal reaction. She missed Robert and what they'd shared. And yet, she was unwilling to go through the torment she'd suffered when he'd died ever again. Nor did she need the sort of confusion in her life right now that men excelled at creating. She wanted to focus on work and nothing else, certainly not on a man without a last name who would only stay in her life for a few short days. She couldn't afford to have Shayde complicate her life. Which meant… Her mouth firmed. Which meant that the minute the popcorn finished, she'd march into the den and give her aggressive employee his marching orders.

The instant she made her decision she felt much better. Upending the contents of the microwaved bag into a bowl, she returned to the den. The tape had just finished the previews and Shayde sat in the middle of the couch, his feet stretched out in front of him. She set the popcorn on the table across from him, but before she could make her grand pronouncement, he wrapped his arm around her waist. She only had a second to gasp out a protest before he tipped her into his arms and stretched out on the couch with her.

Tess started to struggle, then gave it up as futile. If Bull couldn't win a tussle with Shayde, she didn't have a chance. She'd only end up with a bruised dignity. "What do you think you're doing?" she demanded.

"I'm watching a movie with you."

"I watch movies vertically, thank you very much. Besides, I've decided—"

"Really? You don't know what you're missing." He reached for a handful of popcorn. "Relax, Tess."

"I can't. I've decided you should leave."

He nodded, popping some kernels into his mouth. "I pretty much figured you'd reach that decision. Three, four minutes all alone. Smart woman like you. Gives you way too much time to make decisions."

"Is that a crack?"

"Not at all. It's merely predictable. You've been resistant to the idea of hiring me from the start, and yet, you were driven to do it. It has the feel of someone who's tried everything else without success and has decided to go this route as a final, last-ditch option. But it's not a decision you like and so you're fighting for all you're worth to find a way out."

Once again he'd shown an uncanny ability to see what she'd rather keep hidden. She scowled. It wasn't a quality she appreciated. Why couldn't he be cute, but a bit thick? What was so tough about smiling on command, making innocuous chitchat with co-workers and clients, and acting possessive on the few occasions she needed a me-Tarzan, you-Jane throwback hanging on her arm?

"Okay, fine. Stay a little longer," she reluctantly agreed. He shifted his position so they were spooned tightly together and it took every ounce of self-possession to keep from squirming in protest. There was too much of him, and all of it aggressively masculine. Worse, after so many years without a man, everything about Shayde felt alien—the crisp, earthy scent of him, the boldness of his touch, the gravelly rumble of his voice. She struggled to adjust to his strangeness with only limited success. "But I don't see why we can't do this sitting up."

"We can't do this sitting up because holding you is the most effective way for us to become familiar with each other."

"Familiar?" She didn't like the sound of that. "How familiar?"

"Familiar enough that you won't flinch whenever I touch you."

"If I promise not to flinch, will you let me go?"

"Honey, normally I'd take it slow and easy with you. Especially you," he confused her by adding. "But there isn't any time. You want to convince people we're lovers by tomorrow night? Great. I'm the man for the job. But it's not going to happen unless we become comfortable with each other and fast."

"Do I need to point out that I'm not in the least comfortable?"

He exhaled, stirring the hair along the curve of her cheek. She fought to control a shiver of awareness. She wasn't attracted to Shayde. She couldn't be. She was simply tired and stressed and reacting to the flood of male vibes that he exuded with every single breath. All that masculinity made her susceptible. He couldn't help that it had been years since she'd allowed a man to get this close or that her desire to escape his hold conflicted with an equally strong desire to wrap herself around him and become lost in pure lusty pleasure.

"I'm well aware that you're uncomfortable with me," he murmured. "Unless you want everyone else aware of it, too, I suggest you relax. Focus on the movie and ignore me."

Ignore him? Was he kidding? How in the world could she possibly do that? The couch wasn't all that wide and he held her so close she could feel every breath, every heartbeat, every ripple of every muscle. She moistened her lips with the tip of her tongue. "The movie. Right."

"In case you hadn't noticed, that's the moving picture on the television in front of you."

Her mouth curved in a helpless smile. Thank heaven he couldn't see, though knowing him, he probably sensed her amusement. "Thanks for the tip."

He slid his arm from around her waist and grabbed up another helping of popcorn, holding some to her lips. Closing her eyes, she took the proffered treat. She'd never had anyone feed her by hand. There was something earthy about it, something that stripped away inhibition and common sense. But even as she shied from the intimacy, she yielded to it. The butter coating his fingers stained her lips and she couldn't quite suppress a shiver. Getting used to each other was one thing. But this…

Just a single movie. That's all she had to get through. A scant two hours and she'd send him on his way. She'd endured far worse. In fact, that was part of the problem. Having him close didn't feel half bad—and it should. Determined to ignore him, she focused on the romantic comedy he'd selected. One hour and fifty-nine minutes. No sweat.

With one hour and fifty-five minutes remaining,

Shayde reached around her once more, this time for a napkin. "Need one?"

She stared at the screen. For some reason the scintillating dialogue failed to scintillate no matter how hard she concentrated. "No, thanks."

"Popcorn?"

"I'm fine." Giving lie to her words, she squirmed ever so slightly. This was ridiculous. "Are you sure we haven't gotten comfortable enough to convince—"

"Positive. Here…" He eased one arm beneath her so that her head rested in the crook of his shoulder. "How's that?"

Tess cleared her throat. "Fine."

He levered her hips more snugly into the juncture of his. "And this? Better?"

She burned at every contact point. How could that be better? Somehow the connection between them had even affected her vocal chords. It took three tries to get the words out. "Just great."

She wouldn't move again. No matter what he did, no matter how ill at ease she became, she'd endure. Even if every muscle cramped into a thousand knots, she wouldn't so much as twitch.

Or so she thought right up until the clock ticked down to one hour and thirty minutes remaining. Resting his chin against the top of her head, the arm he had draped around her waist shifted. His hand settled in the gap between her jeans and the knit top, and her breath froze in her chest. Slowly his hand splayed across her abdomen, his fingers scorching her skin. She exploded into motion. Leaping from the couch, she whirled around to face him.

"What do you think you're doing?"

He lifted upward onto one elbow. "Watching a movie with my lover. What are you doing?"

"We're not lovers," she bit out. "We aren't now and never will be. How you could think—" She broke off and closed her eyes with a groan. She'd overreacted. Badly. And they both knew it.

"At the risk of sounding repetitive, you don't need to worry about what I think. Just what everyone else will think. And they're going to think that we're two strangers who can barely stand each other. I suggest you come back to the couch, and we'll try this again."

The calm dispassion of his tone got through to her when nothing else would have and she exhaled roughly. "If I do, you'll touch me again."

"You're right. I will. And I'll keep touching you until you stop flinching from me."

"You were touching my stomach." She wished she could see him more clearly, but the lack of lights made that impossible. They allowed him to melt into the shadows, only the silvery glint of his gaze escaping the darkness. It reminded her of the first time they'd met. Then, as now, the sharp awareness in those odd eyes impacted with devastating force. "Were you planning to touch me like that at the party tomorrow night?"

"Only if you're planning to wear something that leaves your midriff bare."

"I won't be."

"Hmm. More's the pity." He patted the space she'd vacated. "Come on, Tess. Let's watch the rest of the movie."

"I think we've done enough for one night."

"Not even close. If anything you've proven how far we have to go. Do you want this to work or don't you? It's your choice."

Damn him! Why did he have to push this? Why all the hassle? They could fake it well enough to get by tomorrow. Didn't he understand? She didn't want a man invading her home. She didn't want him in her kitchen or her den or lounging on her couch like some great jungle cat. She wanted her privacy back. Glancing at the clock, she nearly groaned. One hour and twenty minutes left. It was an eternity. Yanking at the hem of her top, she returned to the couch. What had she been thinking to wear something so provocative? So much for trying to avoid being labeled "elegant." Next time she'd go for head to toe flannel.

He must have read her mind. "You still look elegantly casual even in jeans," he murmured close to her ear.

She returned to the same position as before. For some reason the arm across her waist didn't seem as alien as before. "Don't you mean casually elegant?"

"Not tonight." He brushed her hair from her cheek and traced the curve of her jawline with his fingertip. "It isn't just what you wear. It's how you wear it."

She didn't yank away, but allowed the caress. Worse, she took pleasure in it. She closed her eyes, no longer even pretending that she found the movie absorbing. Had Robert ever touched her this way? If he had, she couldn't remember any longer. As much as she'd loved her husband, he hadn't possessed the sort of innate sensuality that Shayde embodied. She also found it sad that she couldn't remember the tiny details about her life with Robert any longer. After he'd died, she'd thought they were burned into her memory, that she'd never forget. But time had betrayed her. Time had betrayed them both.

For the next hour she managed to accept Shayde's presence with every appearance of equanimity. With only a few minutes left on the clock, she heard his quiet

sigh, felt the air escape his lungs, and knew he would
touch her again.

"Please don't," she whispered into the darkness.

His finger paused just shy of her lips. "Why?"

"I can't—" The words caught in her throat and she
mutely shook her head.

"And I can't help it."

He turned her to face him, sliding a hand down her
spine to the bare hollow at the small of her back. Ever
so gently he pressed, urging her closer. They locked together with delicious perfection. Where had their earlier
clumsiness gone? She'd been more comfortable man-
gling dance steps and sharing awkward kisses than fitting
into his arms as though she belonged. This seemed
frighteningly right and it shouldn't.

He cushioned her with a tenderness she hadn't known
in far too long. He felt good. So good. "Tess—"

Someone needed to remain sensible. To show a modi-
cum of common sense and restraint. Since Shayde didn't
intend to, the job fell to her. "The movie's over now,"
she managed to say. "And so is our evening."

"I don't give a damn about the movie. There's only
one thing I'm interested in doing right now."

She shouldn't ask. She should get off the couch. The
end of the movie offered the perfect excuse. Instead, she
lifted her face to his. "What are you interested in doing?"

"This..."

Shayde cupped Tess's face and took her mouth in a
slow kiss. It was so much better than the one they'd
shared in the kitchen that it defied comparison and he
almost groaned out loud. There he'd been ruled by the
urge to put his stamp on her, a hunter giving chase. But
this time, he just wanted to sink into her. To lose himself

in her eagerness. And she was eager. She didn't hesitate as she had before, but slid her arms around his waist and up along his back.

"Open to me, Tess."

It should have come out as gentle encouragement. Instead, the words held a raspy demand. She reacted instantly and a fierce elation gripped him. There was no shyness. No reluctance or apprehension. She struck him as a woman who set goals and went after them with uncompromising determination.

Her lips parted, welcoming him home and he surged inward, staking a claim. Desire thrummed through him, the insistent beat a cadence that drove him to roll her over and surge between her denim clad thighs. His hand found the gap between the bottom of her shirt and the top of her jeans. Her skin was soft, the muscles of her abdomen rippling beneath his touch. She didn't fight him. Instead, her legs tangled with his and she kneaded his back in open encouragement.

He inched his hands upward beneath her knit top, his fingertips finding pure silk. Her breath escaped in a rush and he drank in the sweet moan. Did she have any idea how intoxicating he found the sound of her...the taste of her...the feel of her? He was supposed to be in total control. But with Tess, one simple kiss destroyed years of effort and training. Everything that was most primitive within him surged to the surface, stripping him of all but the most basic emotions. Want. Need. An overwhelming imperative to mate, to make this woman his and his alone.

"You don't belong to me," he muttered.

She gazed up at him, her eyes hazed with passion. She moistened her swollen lips. "What?"

"We shouldn't be doing this."

She buried her face against his shoulder, shaking. It took a moment to realize she was laughing. "Now you decide we shouldn't be doing this? I thought it was the whole point of the exercise."

"We're supposed to become accustomed to each other's touch. That's all."

"Considering where your hands are right now, I'd say I've become more than accustomed."

When had her bra no longer become a hindrance? He'd filled his hands with her, his thumbs playing across the sensitive tips of her breasts. The scent of her perfumed the air, the silent call of a woman to her lover. She was flushed with warmth and totally open, fitting herself to him with instinctive ease. A hungry eagerness shimmered in the air, a tension building beneath the collapse of her barriers. Whether she recognized the signs or not, she was ready for a man. And not just any man. *Him.*

Shayde shut his eyes. Dammit all! The irony nearly killed him. He'd been working to provoke this sort of response all evening. And now that he had, he couldn't act on it. She wasn't his to take, no matter how badly he wanted her. He'd been a fool to force the relationship this far. If he hadn't been so attracted to her, he'd never have put them in such an untenable situation. But he had and now it was up to him to correct the mistake.

"You're not flinching anymore."

She pretended to consider the matter. "There's a reason for that."

"Could it be that you've gotten comfortable around me?"

"Not even a little."

"But you're physically attracted." There wasn't any

point in phrasing it as a question. They both knew it was the truth.

"I'm afraid so." She caught his wrists and gently pulled. He adjusted her bra and obediently slid his hands from beneath her top. "And I shouldn't be. You're my employee, not my lover."

"Just your pretend lover."

She conceded the observation with a nod. "You've proven your point, Shayde. And you've accomplished what you'd planned. There's an excellent chance I won't flinch the next time you touch me."

"The next time I touch you, I may not be able to let go."

Her eyes dilated, but her voice remained surprisingly steady. "You'll have to. Our relationship is a business one. It can't be more than that."

He levered upward and forced himself off the couch. He couldn't remember the last time he'd found it so difficult to leave the arms of a woman. Perhaps if he'd made love to her, he wouldn't be experiencing this problem. But desire continued to ride him hard, especially when he looked at her spread across the cushions.

Her fiery hair tumbled about her face in unruly waves, an outward expression of the fire burning within. Her arms and legs were still open to him, her position sheer temptation. Even her eyes were those of a woman caught between capricious wishes and painful reality.

Slowly she gathered herself into the woman he'd first met. She straightened her limbs, then her clothing. Even her hair subsided into tidy waves. Impressive. To go from wanton passion to absolute control in the space of a heartbeat spoke of an iron will. She stood and faced him. He sensed her barriers were more fragile than she'd care to admit and that he could surmount them with little effort. But he didn't want her that way. When they came together it would be a conscious decision, not one made in the heat of the moment or through a forced breach in her barriers.

"I'm going to touch you again," he warned. "You realize that, don't you?"

She inclined her head. "You're welcome to in the course of business and in the company of others."

"And when we're alone?"

Her gaze fixed on his without flinching. "There won't be any need to touch, will there?"

"I guess that depends on how well we do in public." Time to let it go. There wasn't any point in pushing her further. He'd succeeded in getting her to open to him. Why give her the excuse to close down? "When do you want me to pick you up tomorrow?"

"The benefit begins at seven. Dinner's included."

"I'll pick you up at six-fifteen."

"Oh, and Shayde?" For the first time she showed a hint of hesitation. "It's formal. Will that be a problem?"

"Not for me." He should leave. Instead, he returned to her side. Sliding a hand around her neck, he tipped her chin up with his thumb. "Good night, Tess. I know how tough this has been on you. Thank you for trying."

She did precisely the wrong thing. Lifting up, she joined her mouth with his. Her kiss spoke of all that she denied, whispering words she'd never have dared utter. She told him he affected her in ways no man ever had before, that no matter how hard she tried, she couldn't resist his touch, that she wanted him with a desperation she couldn't fully hide. He matched all she had to give him with silent words of his own. In that one delicious melding he told her that she was the most beautiful woman he'd ever held, the sweetest he'd ever tasted, the most desirable, most passionate, the most unique.

With a murmur of regret, she ended the kiss with unmistakable finality. "Goodbye, Shayde."

He didn't let her get away with such a final dismissal. "Until next time."

If the words sounded like a warning, perhaps that was because they were. No matter what it took, he'd have Tess in his arms again. And soon.

CHAPTER FIVE

THE minute Tess heard the front door close, she sank onto the couch and dropped her head into her hands. What in the name of heaven had she done? She'd allowed a complete stranger to touch her as intimately as a lover. Not only had she accepted his kisses and caresses, but she'd thoroughly enjoyed them.

"Either I've turned into a frustrated old maid or it's been too long since I've been with a man."

Both observations hit a little too close to home. It *had* been too long since she'd made love. Nine long, lonely years. Until tonight she'd never felt the need to take another man into her bed. Not after Robert. No one had ever attracted her as fiercely as her late husband. But Shayde stirred emotions she'd thought long dead, and it disturbed her.

A lot.

She didn't want to feel this way about a man again. Losing Robert had been the worst experience of her life, one from which she hadn't expected to ever recover. As a result, she'd thrown all her time and energy into her job. Now that she was on the brink of becoming the youngest vice president in the company, she wasn't about to jeopardize that for anyone or anything. And Shayde did threaten to jeopardize her promotion by distracting her at such a key moment in her career. Besides, what did he have to offer? A quick, meaningless romp in the sack, that's all.

Slowly she straightened, her hands dropping to her

lap. She wasn't interested in Shayde as a man, she told herself firmly. Her mouth compressed. No. She didn't care about his personality or his background or what circumstances made him the man he was today. Her interest didn't spring from such a noble source, but from a far more earthy one. It came from sheer physical desire and how he made her feel when he touched her.

Well, those needs could be suppressed if not extinguished, at least for the length of time it would take to complete her association with him. Now that she'd made her decision, she'd take herself off to bed. By morning she'd have herself under control once again. She started to leave the couch, then hesitated.

Unable to explain what possessed her, she curled up on the cushions. Shayde's scent filled her nostrils and she shut her eyes, shivering. She should go to bed and get as far as possible from the images provoked by the past few hours. Instead, she sank deeper into cushions still bearing the warmth of Shayde's body and relived every minute she'd spent in his arms. If she couldn't have the man, she'd have the memories.

Wrapped in his lingering traces, she allowed sleep to claim her.

He was an idiot.

Shayde paced through the streets of Seattle, hoping the exercise would help him regain control. What the *hell* had he been thinking? It was one thing to rationalize his actions so far—at least the ones right up until he'd pulled Tess onto that couch and done his level best to make her his own. He could claim he was putting her in touch with her feminine side. Reminding her of how men and women were supposed to interact. But she wasn't for him. He was supposed to be instigating a romance between her and the Committee's choice, and trying to get the delectable Mrs. Lonigan out of her clothes probably wasn't the best way of doing that.

That didn't change the simple fact that he wanted her. Man, did he want her.

His cell phone trilled and he snapped it open. "Shayde."

"I require an update on the Lonigan project."

He grimaced. Just what he needed to top off his evening, a call from the dragon lady. "And how are you this picture-perfect evening, boss?"

"Immaterial." Gee, that came as a surprise. When had personal chitchat ever overridden her focus on business? "I believe I requested a status report."

A status report on Tess Lonigan. Let's see... She's the softest, most delectable woman he'd ever had the pleasure of touching. The passion of her kisses drove every other thought from his head and he'd have paid any price to strip away her clothing and make love to her until they were both sated. Somehow he doubted his employer would appreciate his including those details in a report. "Tess is coming along," he limited himself to saying.

"Explain."

"She may be ready for a man."

"Explain." The word no longer came as a request, but as a demand.

Shadoe chose that moment to join in the conversation. "That doesn't sound like the job we assigned you, little brother. What have you been up to?"

Shayde winced. Perhaps he should have been more cautious in his wording. "I mean that when we first met, her only concern was business. That may have changed."

The boss lady took over the conversation again. "How has it changed?"

"She seems more open to a relationship," he grudgingly admitted.

"How do you know?"

Was she kidding? "Come on. A man can tell."

"We had this discussion," Shadoe interrupted. "Tess is not for you."

Inexplicable anger rippled through Shayde. "You shouldn't keep saying that," he advised through gritted teeth. "Telling a man he can't have something makes him all the more determined to get it."

"Forget it, bro. You can't have Tess Lonigan."

Shayde paused beneath the protection of a Japanese umbrella pine and shook the dampness from his hair. "You want an update?" he snarled. "Here's your update. The lady is focused on her career. She doesn't have any use or need for a man other than as a way up the corporate ladder. At a guess, she's still in love with her late husband. At the very least, she's sexually frustrated which isn't the best foundation for marriage. Happy?"

Shadoe refused to be drawn. "Tomorrow night you'll introduce her to the man selected for her. Any questions?"

"Yeah, I have a question. A big one. She didn't ask the Committee for help finding a husband. She asked for help finding husbands for her friends. Why are we interfering in Tess's life?"

"Her brother put her name on our list before she ever approached the Committee. It was sheer coincidence that she came seeking a match for Emma and Raine."

Hell. He was going to strangle Seth. "Why would Tess's own brother do that to her?"

"Don't you think she deserves to be happy?" Shadoe asked mildly.

"Deserves? It sounds more like a punishment to me."

"Just because you consider marriage a punishment doesn't mean everyone agrees with your assessment. Tess obviously doesn't, otherwise she wouldn't ask our help finding husbands for her friends."

As much as Shayde wanted to rail against such a logical conclusion, he couldn't. Besides, why fight the inevitable? They'd already reminded him the Committee never made a mistake. He'd seen them in action, seen how well their choices had worked in the past. Whomever they'd selected as Prince to Tess's Cinderella, must be the perfect man for her. Right?

"So who is this joker, anyway?" he reluctantly asked.

Shadoe's boss took over the conversation. "She already knows the man. So do you for that matter, which is why you were chosen for this job. The preliminary data on him has been sent to you by E-mail. All you need to do is instigate the romance."

"Just stick them together and let nature take its course?"

"That would be acceptable," she confirmed

"Fine. I'll start tomorrow. Anything else?"

It was Shadoe's turn for a parting shot. "One final suggestion.... Do your job."

There wasn't anything more to be said. Flipping the phone closed, Shayde pocketed it and glared out at the deserted streets. Oh, he'd do his job, just as he always had. But never before had he felt such aversion to a simple matchmaking project. Perhaps when he met this prince Shadoe had uncovered, he'd change his mind. Perhaps he'd concede that the two were a perfect match. But somehow he doubted it. When he thought about how she'd reacted when in his arms, how she'd opened herself to him, and how eagerly her lips had parted beneath his, he more than doubted it. He was absolutely positive the Committee was wrong.

And he'd do everything in his power to prove it.

Shayde arrived promptly at six-fifteen. Tess opened the door and he fought to hide his reaction. She looked stunning. She wore a simple ivory shift that clung to every incredible curve and she'd topped it with a short bolero-style jacket covered in swirls of glittering beadwork. The color set off her pale skin and vivid hair, and turned her eyes a riveting shade of blue. She wore her hair up and had added to her height with a pair of three-inch heels. She'd also shrouded herself in a cool, remote air that would have done an ice princess proud.

"You're beautiful, Tess," he said. He deliberately invaded her space and kissed her.

She pleased him by swaying toward him, relaxing into the embrace. An unmistakable tension hummed between them and her breathing kicked up a notch. Her reaction didn't come from nervousness, but awareness, and was exactly the sort of undercurrent he hoped her co-workers would sense. As though she'd picked up on it, as well, Tess took a careful step backward, fortifying her barriers with impressive speed.

"I won't tell," he murmured.

She lifted an eyebrow in question. "Excuse me?"

He couldn't resist teasing. "I won't tell anyone that you slipped up when I touched you. It can be our little secret."

Annoyance fought with amusement and after an endless second her mouth twitched and a laugh escaped. "You're impossible."

"So I've been told," he sympathized.

She regarded him for a frustrated moment, clearly uncertain how to deal with him. "I made up my mind after you left last night that I wouldn't let you get to me again."

He couldn't resist touching her once more, tracing the smooth line of her neck from her elegant jawline to the tempting hollow at the base of her throat. "Don't feel bad. You held out for a whole thirty seconds."

Her amusement faded. "Five," she whispered. "It only took five."

Hell. The muscles in his jaw flexed. They really were in trouble. "If we don't get out of here now, we're not going."

Crossing to a hallway table, she picked up a purse that could have passed as a postage stamp and gestured toward the door. "Shall we?" she asked formally. "I don't want to be late."

No. Shayde didn't, either. He was in a hurry to find Tess's future husband and instigate a romance between them. And then he'd be out of her life and she'd get her happily-ever-after ending. They'd both be satisfied. She'd go her way and he'd go his. He followed her out the door, unable to take his eyes off the tempting sway of her hips. Joining her on the sidewalk, he wrapped an arm around her and tucked her close. Yeah, he'd go his.

Eventually.

They made the trip downtown in silence. Aside from an uplifted eyebrow and a swift, speculative glance, Tess didn't comment on Shayde's Jaguar. It was just as well. He doubted he'd have been able to lie to her about how he'd afforded it on the sort of salary he'd earn through a temporary employment agency. Unfortunately, the truth would lead to more questions than he cared to answer at this point. How did he explain that he spent most days managing the fortune he'd earned in the stock market whenever he wasn't moonlighting as an Instigator? Somehow he doubted that would go over well.

They arrived at the cancer benefit early and she took the time to introduce him to her co-workers, as well as her boss. Al Portman was a large jovial man with shrewd, intelligent eyes and Shayde suspected it would take a stellar performance to convince this man they shared an intimate involvement. The dancing started not long after they'd made the rounds and Shayde slipped an arm around Tess, walking with her toward the dance floor.

"Time to start the show," he murmured close to her ear.

To his relief, she didn't pull away, but accepted the light embrace. His hold tightened and he skimmed his hand along her spine. She felt incredible, fitting against him as though she belonged. At least, she did right up until they began to dance. As he took the first few steps across the floor, Tess glanced up at him. The instant their eyes met, she stumbled.

Her reaction to the mistake didn't help. She went rigid, her expression turning alarmed. "I don't know if I can do this."

"Sure you can," he soothed, sticking to the most elementary of steps.

"Please, Shayde." The words came in a panicked whisper. "I told you I didn't want to dance with you again."

"I remember. I also warned that we'd only get one shot at this."

"In that case, we'd better get off the floor or I'll ruin everything."

"Relax, sweetheart. You're not going to ruin a thing. We're going to dance just like we did last night."

She tromped on his toe. She'd also done that the night before, but he'd hoped she'd forgotten that particular maneuver. It would appear she hadn't. "See? It's not working. We have to change the plan." She moistened her lips, desperation flickering in her gaze. "I'll—I'll pretend to twist my ankle. You can help me off the floor and we won't need to dance for the rest of the night."

"Calm down, Tess." It was now or never. If he couldn't convince her to play her role in a convincing manner during their first dance, everything they'd worked to accomplish would go right down the tubes. "Close your eyes," he ordered.

"What?"

"Close your eyes." He barked his instructions in a gruff undertone, knowing it was the only way to get through to her. "Do it. Now."

Her lashes flickered downward. "What next?" she asked stiffly.

"Listen to my voice. Feel me moving against you and pretend we're back in your hallway. That we're all alone." She missed one last step and then magically, her movements matched his. "That's right. Just keep focusing on me and nothing else. I won't let you down. I won't desert you. And I'm going to do everything in my power to help you get this promotion. Trust me, Tess."

Her laugh held a shaky quality. "You sure know how to sweet-talk a woman."

"It's not sweet talk," he denied. "I'm being dead honest."

"I wish I could believe you."

"You can." He needed to distract her so she wouldn't have time to think about what they were doing. "I have to tell you, Tess. This doesn't make sense to me. You're a strong woman. Determined. Focused. How is it possible that one simple dance could rattle you so badly?''

''It's all your fault.''

''*My* fault?'' Perfect. Annoyance had replaced her earlier self-consciousness. Maybe if he kept pushing her buttons, she'd continue dancing like an angel. ''How do you figure?''

She opened one eye long enough to peek up at him. ''It's a perfectly logical conclusion. I don't have this problem with anyone else. Therefore it has to be your fault.''

''Got it. All the other men you've danced with before were total wusses who let you lead.''

''That's not what I meant.''

He cautiously molded her closer. ''I'll bet they didn't hold you like this, though, did they? Not even for show.''

She shivered, winding her arms around his neck. ''Are you positive this is just for show?''

He buried a smile against the top of her head. Finally. The perfection they'd experienced in the hallway returned, their movements as intimately matched as lovers. ''For both our sakes, it had better be.''

She opened her eyes and regarded him seriously. ''Then you agree with my original proposal?''

''Which proposal was that?''

Her fingers slid along the nape of neck and into his hair. It was all he could do to keep from groaning. ''You promised we would maintain a professional distance, remember?''

''Yeah. A professional distance. Whatever you say, lady.''

She massaged his scalp in slow, hypnotic circles. "Am I putting on a good enough act?"

He pulled back slightly so he could glance down at her, allowing his amusement to ease into his expression. "Is that what you're doing? Putting on an act?"

There was something about a slow smile coming from a blue-eyed redhead that was as sultry as hell. "What else could it be?"

"Oh, I don't know." He swept a stray curl from her temple as he drifted with her across the floor. "The real thing?"

Her smile grew. "Not a chance. You told me we have to be convincing tonight. You also told me last night that we'd only get one shot at this. It's amazing what a little motivation will do for a woman."

"You're certainly doing an excellent job convincing your co-workers we're serious. They haven't taken their eyes off us since we hit the dance floor."

"Do they look like they're buying our performance?"

"Hell, sweetheart. I'm buying it." He feathered a kiss along her jawline. "Why wouldn't they?"

To his disappointment, her hands slid from his hair and settled onto his shoulders. "Don't overdo it, Shayde," she warned. "You'll make me nervous. And you know what happens when I get nervous."

"You mean how you flinch and flutter and get all skittish around me?"

"That's not quite how I'd phrase it." She shrugged. "But it's not worth arguing over semantics. We've done a good job convincing everyone that we're serious. I don't want to do anything that'll change that."

"You mean, for instance, if I were to hold you too close." He deliberately locked her hips against his. "What might happen if I did that?"

She moistened her lips and he took an unwarranted amount of satisfaction in the fact that it took her two tries to formulate a reply. "I might do some of that flinching and fluttering."

"Really?" He pretended to consider. "We wouldn't want that."

She shook her head and a few more curls floated free from the formal knot at the nape of her neck. They settled along the curve of her cheekbones, the fiery ringlets a brilliant contrast to her creamy skin. "No, we wouldn't."

"How about if I were to steal a kiss, instead?" He took her mouth in a lingering caress, thoroughly enjoying the taste of her. "What might happen then?"

Her pulse kicked up a notch, throbbing beneath his hands. "I'd end the dance."

"Bad idea," he murmured. "Your clients might get suspicious."

She cleared her throat. "And that would defeat the whole purpose of the exercise."

"I guess that means I shouldn't kiss you."

"I really rather you didn't."

He chuckled at the brazen lie. "I suppose that just leaves us with a plain, simple old-fashioned dance."

"It would..." She shot him a look from beneath her lashes. "Except for one small problem."

"And what's that?"

"There isn't anything plain or simple—let alone old-fashioned—about the way you dance."

He grinned. "I would hope not."

Scooping her closer, he swung her around the floor, taking pleasure in the blatantly seductive movements. She felt incredible in his arms. Warm. Alive. Willing.

Hell, she was more than willing, which created a definite problem.

He could invent all the excuses in the world about opening her up in order to reignite her interest in men. But the simple truth was that he wanted her—and not for anything noble like marriage. He wanted the woman in his bed, her hot-sun curls tumbling across his pillow while she wrapped those pale, silken limbs around him in a lover's embrace. He wanted her mouth beneath his, every inch of her closed around every inch of him, and her satisfaction ringing in his ears. Nothing less would do.

She wasn't meant for him.

The words came out of nowhere, no doubt summoned by the commitment he'd made to his brother. Dammit all! He'd never broken his word before. And no matter how hard he fought the truth, the hard, cold fact was that somewhere at this party he'd find the man the Committee had chosen for Tess. The ''perfect'' man. The man who would give the woman in his arms her fairy tale ending. And then his true job would begin. He'd have to find ways to instigate a relationship, regardless of her preferences—his mouth tightened—or his.

Tess's hand tightened on his shoulder. ''What's wrong, Shayde?''

He glided to a stop on the far side of the dance floor. ''Sorry?''

''You look like you're a thousand miles away.''

He should release her now that they'd stopped dancing. Ignoring every rational impulse, his arms tightened around her. ''I was lost in my own thoughts.''

She leaned into his embrace, her head close to his.

"Judging by your expression they weren't pleasant ones. Anything you'd like to share?"

"An obligation I'd rather avoid."

Tess nodded in perfect understanding. "I know all about obligations. Particularly the unpleasant sort. Is this one job related?"

Before he could answer Al Portman approached. "Excuse me for interrupting," he said with a broad smile. "We're about to go in to dinner. Afterward, Tess, I'll be assigning you an Impossible."

"I look forward to it," she replied.

Something in her tone warned Shayde that she was lying. Considering her drive and determination to win the promotion he couldn't help wondering at her reluctance. "What's wrong?" he asked quietly as they headed for the dining room.

"I think I know who Al has chosen for me."

"And?"

"And if I'm right about his choice, I don't have a chance of getting this promotion."

"Why?"

"Let's just say there are personal complications that are interfering with my soliciting him for business purposes."

"Personal complications, as in…romantic sort of complications?"

"You're very good at this, Shayde."

"The best."

He was also very good at reading between the lines. This Impossible had been putting the moves on her. Maybe he'd even offered to make a generous donation to Altruistics in exchange for an equally generous donation on Tess's part. And her solution had been to hire someone to play the part of her lover in order to fend off his unwanted advances.

Shayde fought to keep his voice level. Not that he succeeded. It grated even more than normal. "How can I help?" Aside from beat the bastard to a bloody pulp, he barely refrained from adding. Probably just as well he didn't mention that option to Tess. She might try and talk him out of it.

Her gaze flickered in his direction and the expression he read there did little to cool his anger. "Stay close," she murmured.

"This man you're concerned about, he's the reason you hired me, isn't he?

"Yes."

"And I'm supposed to send out signals that you're unavailable romantically so he'll keep his damn hands off you when you approach him about a donation. Is that it?"

She didn't look his way, but her expression gave him all the answer he needed. That tore it! The minute he got Tess alone, he'd find out the name of this guy and precisely how he'd expressed his "interest" in her. And then Shayde planned to track the slimeball down and explain how he'd better not express that sort of interest ever again unless he wanted to lose a few teeth.

Shayde shook his head in disgust. Just great. Maybe he could also thump his chest a few times, let out a blood-curdling bellow, and take a swing from the nearest jungle vine. Of course... Now that he thought about it, there was another possibility. There was an outside chance that this SOB was the same man the Committee had matched with Tess. He grinned. Oh, yeah. He liked that idea.

Unfortunately, it was a one in a million shot, mainly

because Shayde knew the man who'd been chosen for Tess and Grayson Shaw wasn't the kind of guy who'd pull the sort of despicable stunt she'd described. But still… A man could hope. Maybe Gray had turned into a total jerk in the week since they'd last seen each other.

If his insane guess proved accurate, he'd take great delight in planting his fist in Gray's chin before putting a fast end to the Committee's first mismatch. And while he was at it, he might take a minute or two to rub Shadoe's nose in his mistake. Just as a friendly, brotherly gesture. And then… He glanced down at the woman at his side.

And then Tess would be all his.

CHAPTER SIX

ADELAIDE SMITH wasn't at dinner and Tess couldn't decide whether to be relieved or annoyed. Here she'd gone to all the trouble of hiring Shayde, and for what? The whole point of the exercise had been to stop any future matchmaking. That would prove difficult if she couldn't act like a lovelorn idiot in front of the woman who'd made the entire exercise necessary. The only positive that might come from Adelaide's absence was that by not having to deal with her, Tess also wouldn't have to deal with any mercenary sons.

After dinner, Tess made a point of circulating among both clients and benefactors, keeping an eye out for Adelaide while she waited for Al Portman to tell her which Impossible she'd been assigned. Eventually, she found herself standing beside Grayson Shaw, whose name appeared on the list of potential donors just beneath the Smiths.

To her surprise, Shayde offered his hand. "How's it going, Gray?"

"Not bad. And yourself?"

"I'm managing."

Tess glanced from one man to the other. "You two have met before?"

Grayson hesitated for a moment. "We've had dealings."

Tess turned on Shayde. "You know the most interesting people."

"Interesting?" He smiled blandly. "Don't let Gray

fool you. He can be downright dull when he starts in about business.''

Gray accepted the comment without protest. "Guilty as charged.''

Somehow Tess doubted that. There was a confident sophistication about the man that told her he'd never bore a woman. If she were honest, she'd admit she'd liked Grayson Shaw from the start. She'd always found him elegantly handsome and that hadn't changed in the year since they'd first met. Some might even call him austere, perhaps because he seemed so self-contained. But the humor she'd caught in his calm gaze, as well as the way he dealt with people, suggested that even though he was accustomed to taking charge, he remained considerate of those around him. Or maybe she liked him so much simply because he reminded her of Robert.

"Tell me something, Gray.'' An odd look gleamed in Shayde's eyes, a fierce challenge that had Tess staring in alarm. "When people approach you at a shindig like this and try and solicit a donation, have you ever tried to mix business with pleasure?''

The breath escaped Tess's lungs in a rush. Oh, no. He'd totally misunderstood what she'd told him earlier. She opened her mouth to say something that would salvage the situation, but only a strangled squeak escaped. Frantically, she shook her head.

Gray lifted an eyebrow. "Come again?''

"You know… You do me a favor and I'll do you one. Only first you have to get naked.''

Another squeak escaped from Tess, higher this time.

"You propositioning me, old friend?'' Gray questioned mildly.

"*No!*'' Shayde scowled. "I meant with a woman, as you damn well know.''

A spark of anger gleamed in Gray's eyes until he glanced at Tess. From the amount of heat pouring off her face, she suspected her cheeks were flame-red. And she'd bet everything she owned she appeared as panic-stricken as a deer surrounded by gun-toting hunters one minute before the opening of hunting season. Amused speculation replaced his annoyance. "Naked, huh? Think it would work?" He pretended to consider the possibility. "I have to admit, I've never thought to use that method when doing business before."

"You sure?" Shayde looked disappointed. "Never? Not even a loosened tie accompanied by a halfhearted pass? A wink? A smile? Nothing that could be misconstrued?"

Gray turned to Tess. "What do you say, Mrs. Lonigan? Have I been sending out unconscious signals? Stripping down without realizing it? Leering, maybe?" His brows drew together. "I seem to remember smiling on occasion. But unless my eye twitches without my realizing it, I don't ever recall winking."

"No, Mr. Shaw. You've never done anything—" she swiveled to glare at Shayde "—*anything* the least inappropriate the few times we've had dealings."

Shayde didn't bother to hide his disappointment. "You sure?"

"Positive." The music began again and Tess held out her hand to Gray. "I'm suddenly in desperate need of a dance."

To her relief, he took the hint. "If I promise not to mix business with pleasure, would you care to join me?"

"Thank you. I'd love to."

She shot Shayde an exasperated glance over Gray's shoulder, surprised to see he looked less than pleased with her actions. "Behave yourself," she mouthed. "He's an Impossible."

They danced in silence for a minute or two and Tess discovered that the awkwardness she'd experienced with Shayde the first time they'd danced didn't occur with Gray. She fit comfortably in his arms, matching her steps to his with instinctive ease. And not once did she trip or stumble or flinch. Of course, her heart didn't beat fast enough to choke her. Nor did she have the overwhelming urge to drag him into the nearest bedroom and make sweet, wild love to him as she had with Shayde. That might be for the best, especially considering the discussion that had just occurred between the two men.

"Devising a way to achieve world peace?"

Tess blinked up at Gray in total confusion. "Excuse me?"

"You seemed lost in thought and I was trying to break the ice." He shrugged, his blue eyes alight with humor. "I see I've failed miserably."

"I'm sorry, Gray. I was thinking about—" Oh, dear. Another blush swept like wildfire across her cheekbones. "I was thinking—"

He smoothed over the awkward pause with a charming smile. "Don't worry about Shayde. He and I are old friends. I gather you've been having trouble with someone trying to mix business with pleasure?"

She nodded. "It's so ridiculous. Just a small matchmaking attempt that's gotten a little out of hand. Shayde completely misunderstood the situation."

"That's a surprise. He's usually more subtle." Gray fixed her with a speculative look before changing the subject, much to Tess's relief. "I believe we have a mutual friend. Emma Palmer?"

"She and I were at college together." Tess relaxed ever so slightly. "We've been friends for ages."

"Emma and I have known each other for more years than she'd care to admit. I made the connection between you a couple of weeks ago when I saw a picture of the two of you sitting on a fence with a dark-haired woman."

"That would be Raine Featherstone. The photo was taken at her ranch in Texas the summer she and Emma graduated from college. We all have a copy of that snapshot." Tess smiled at the memory of those carefree days. "I haven't gotten down to San Francisco for a visit in months. How is Emma?"

"Wayward," he stated succinctly.

Tess took a moment to digest that. "I've never heard that word used to describe her before, but it suits, I think. She's always been a free spirit."

"You mean she's always gone her own way without thought or consideration for how her actions affect those around her."

Tess couldn't help laughing. "I see you know Emma well."

"Too well. I've had the pleasure of Emma's companionship since she was the size of a mosquito and swathed in diapers." He tilted his head to one side. "As I recall she used to climb out of them at every possible opportunity."

"She looks like such a sweet, innocent thing and yet she's the most stubborn of us all."

Gray swung her in a quick circle. "I've learned from painful experience that Emma Palmer could outstubborn a herd of donkeys."

"That's our Emma," Tess concurred with a wide grin.

*   *   *

Shayde paced on the sidelines, glaring at Tess. Not that she noticed. Hell, no. Ms. Touch-Me-Not had turned into a veritable clinging vine. Not only did she fit in Grayson Shaw's arms with a perfection that drew whispered comments from around the room, but she'd looked relaxed and natural. Dammit, she even laughed. His jaw jutted out. She hadn't laughed when they'd danced.

Gray spun her in a circle, the steps more complicated than any Shayde had seen her perform to date. She followed with ease. Not once did she attempt to lead, nor did she hold her partner at a distance. Instead, she pressed every luscious curve into every masculine angle with a familiarity that had Shayde slamming his back teeth together. *This?* This was the man his brother thought a perfect match for Tess, Mr. Suave and Sophisticated mated with Mrs. Cool and Businesslike?

He silently steamed. It galled him that Shadoe could be right. They matched like a pair of damned bookends.

Why couldn't Gray have been the man Tess had been trying to avoid? Shayde balled his hands into fists. It would have made everything so simple. That way he could have told the Committee to take a flying leap. He could have told Gray to take a flying leap, too. And maybe, just maybe, he could have gotten out of the situation without looking like a total jackass.

The dance ended then and Tess and Gray approached. Shayde forced his mouth into as close to a smile as he could manage. Not that it fooled Tess. After a minute of stilted conversation, Gray excused himself with a knowing grin. The instant he was out of earshot, Tess turned on Shayde, practically vibrating with anger.

"What?" she demanded. "What's wrong?"

He trotted out the easiest response given the circumstances—a total lie. "Nothing's wrong."

"Don't give me that. You're doing one of those man things and I want to know why."

Good. He'd been spoiling for a fight. Gray hadn't been willing to oblige. It looked like he might get one, after all, and from a more enjoyable source. "What man thing?"

"You know." She waved her hand in the air as though it would grant instant comprehension. "That bristly, someone's dared to set their tippytoe on my territory and I'm going to snort and snarl and growl like a lovesick lion. *Those* sort of man things. Is this because you made a total idiot of yourself with Gray?"

"I did *not* make a total idiot of myself with him." He wouldn't deign to address her lovesick lion comment, perhaps because it was more accurate than he cared to admit. "I made a slight idiot of myself."

"Keep telling yourself that if it'll make you feel better. If you're not all in a twist because of your conversation with Gray, it must be because I danced with him."

"Don't be ridiculous. Why would that bother me?" Maybe if she hadn't done one of those woman things— crossing her arms across her chest and lifting an eyebrow in blatant disbelief—he wouldn't have lost it and ended up proving he was the idiot she'd claimed. "You didn't flinch!"

"Excuse me?"

For the first time in memory, his control completely evaporated. "Why do women always do that? They say 'excuse me' or 'I beg your pardon' in this I-don't-have-a-clue-*what*-you're-talking-about tone of voice when they really know damn well what men mean. You just want us to use all these words to explain ourselves so we end up looking like total fools.''

Her mouth twitched. "It works, doesn't it?"

A red haze drifted across his eyes. "Well, I'm not going to fall for it.'' His voice rumbled like an avalanche of rocks plunging pell-mell down a mountainside. "You didn't flinch when you were dancing with Shaw and you know damn well what I mean.''

"You wanted me to flinch?''

His jaw inched out again. "You did with me. Not only did you flinch, but you fluttered. You also tripped and stumbled and could barely dance once around the room. Now what's with that?''

"I guess it means I'm not attracted to Grayson Shaw.''

He started to say something, then stopped. Well, shoot. He could only think of one response to that. Grasping her arm, he hustled her away from the dance floor and around a corner where they were no longer in public view. Pulling her into his arms, he kissed her. Her mouth blossomed beneath his, open and eager and hungry. Where had the hesitation gone? Where was the awkwardness? They weren't meant for each other and yet it felt so right. How could something this good be a mistake?

The desire he'd teased free last night erupted with stunning force. There was no mistaking the depth of her passion. She didn't attempt to control or hide it any longer and a tiny sound escaped her throat, an urgent murmur of want. She was a woman of contrasts, her body soft against his, but also containing a vibrant tension that underscored her need. He found it an explosive combination, a subtle push and pull, a yielding and yet a demand. He slid his hands beneath her bolero jacket, coaxing free another of the feminine moans that roused all that was most masculine in him.

He wanted her. Now. Regardless of time or place or consequence.

"Mrs. Lonigan?" an incredulous voice interrupted.

Shayde turned swiftly, blocking Tess from view behind the width of his shoulders. Al Portman stood less than five feet away, a disapproving frown lining his brow. "I'm sorry," Shayde said. "We didn't realize anyone was nearby."

"Obviously," the older man replied stiffly. "Nevertheless, I hardly think this is an appropriate venue for that sort of behavior."

He had to act. Now. Only one solution occurred to him, one guaranteed to correct the situation. Unfortunately, it was also guaranteed to infuriate Tess, not to mention Shadoe. Not that Shayde cared about his brother's response. If he didn't repair the damage he'd done to Tess's career, he'd never forgive himself. "You're right. I should have waited to propose marriage until after the benefit. It's entirely my fault."

A fist thudded against his back and he absorbed it with barely a grunt. "How could you?" she bit out in an undertone.

Shayde dropped his arm around Tess's shoulders and eased her forward. He wished he could have given her more opportunity to pull herself together. Although she managed an air of calm, her mouth was bare of lipstick and swollen from his kisses. And her face still wore the hectic flush of a woman caught in the throes of passion. Considering the importance of tonight's benefit and its potential effect on her career, offending her boss probably wasn't the best way to kick off the evening.

"Proposed?" Portman repeated.

Shayde inclined his head. "Again, I apologize. I should have waited until a more appropriate time."

"Not at all." Portman beamed. "Congratulations, Tess. I can't tell you how pleased I am for you. I know how tough it's been on you since Robert's death."

"Thank you," she murmured.

"Now that I understand what I've walked in on, I'm sorry I interrupted." Portman took a quick step backward. "As you know, I'd planned to assign you an Impossible tonight, but how about if we wait for a more convenient time?"

Tess stepped free of Shayde's arms. "Right now is as convenient as any," she replied with an easy shrug.

He lent his support with an encouraging nod. "We don't mind in the least."

Portman hesitated. "If you're certain, I'd be happy to give you the names I've chosen."

She looked visibly startled. "You're giving me more than one Impossible?"

"You'll only have to turn one of them," he was quick to assure. "I have to admit, I'd originally planned to assign a single name—Dick Smith—and see what you could accomplish on that front."

Tension vibrated through Tess. "I'd assumed as much," she replied. Though her voice remained tranquil enough to fool Portman, Shayde caught the underlying dismay. "What changed your mind?"

As she spoke, Tess slipped her hand into the crook of Shayde's arm. He couldn't remember her ever initiating contact between them before. He wondered if she even realized what she'd done. Somehow he doubted it, which meant that something her employer had said had rattled her. Badly. He suspected it was related to Dick Smith, but surely that couldn't be the man she was worried about? Hell. This grew more complicated by the minute.

Her boss tilted his head to one side. "After giving it further thought, it seems more equitable this way. So I'll add Shaw to the list. You seem to have established a rapport with him tonight. That should give you a slight edge." He smiled expansively. "Consider it my engagement present. And for a third choice.... How about Walt Moore?"

"That sounds fine, thanks," Tess replied. "I'll do my best to turn one of them into an active benefactor."

"I'm sure you will. I think this should make for an excellent test of your abilities." Portman held out his hand to Shayde. "Congratulations. You've chosen a wonderful woman. We're all very fond of Tess."

Shayde shook his head. "I think you have that backward. Tess makes her own choices. I'm just lucky to be one of them."

"You're right about that," Portman said with a chuckle. "If you'll excuse me, I'll return to the party. I gather you don't mind if I spread the good news?"

Shayde tried not to wince as Tess dug her nails into his arm. "Not at all," she claimed. She even managed to cap the lie with a sunny smile. "It's just all so unexpected. I thought tonight would be work-related. I'd hate to have my news interfere with that."

Portman didn't pick up on the hint. "On the contrary. I suspect it'll put everyone in a more generous mood." He rubbed his hands together. "We can certainly hope."

The minute he left, Tess swiveled to face Shayde. She never should have hired him. What could she have been thinking? Maybe that was part of the problem. She hadn't been thinking, but reacting to a slew of out-of-control hormones. Well, no longer. Any attraction she felt for him stopped here and now.

All she had to do was figure out how.

"Have you lost your mind?" she demanded.

"I just knew it." He thrust a hand through his hair, ruffling the waves into attractive disorder. Not that she paid it the least attention. Goodness, no. She'd stopped noticing such things a full two seconds ago. "Why am I not surprised? I save your pretty backside from disaster and you give me hell about it. Let me guess. You don't approve of the way I handled the situation."

How could he think otherwise? "Considering you created the situation in the first place, no. I don't approve of how you handled it. Not even a little."

"You'd rather have your boss upset with you for kissing me when you should have been working?"

Didn't he understand? "That's not the point. It should have been my decision, not yours. It's my job that's at stake, in case you've forgotten."

"Granted. But I doubt any other explanation would have worked. You were caught in a compromising situation on the eve of a vital promotion. I bailed you out the best way I knew how."

"Unfortunately, your best has made everything more awkward." She glanced over her shoulder, checking that no one could accidentally overhear their conversation. Though she didn't see anyone within earshot, she lowered her voice, to be on the safe side. "You keep forgetting that I hired you to play a part. It's a temporary position. This is going to complicate matters. How do I explain your disappearance when the job ends?"

"You look brave and stoic and tell everyone that it didn't work out. I wasn't the man you thought. You can either be the dumpee or the dumper depending on which you think would work to your advantage. Until then I'll be available whenever you need me.''

"This isn't what I'd planned.''

"Here's a newsflash. It wasn't what I'd planned, either. We'll just have to—'' He broke off abruptly, staring at something over her shoulder. "How much longer do we have to stay here?'' he asked unexpectedly.

"We can leave anytime, I guess. We'll have to run the gamut of clients and co-workers on our way out the door thanks to Al's announcement.'' Shayde cupped her elbow and urged her into the ballroom. The swift pace caused curls to escape the knot at the nape of her neck and tumble about her cheeks. No doubt Shayde's impassioned kiss hadn't helped. She had a vague recollection of his hands sliding into her hair, loosening the clips. "Why? What's wrong?''

"Have you accomplished what you wanted tonight?'' His voice contained a growing urgency. "Anyone else we need to talk to?''

"I've touched bases with Gray. Dick Smith and Walt Moore aren't here, so I can't make any headway with them.''

"Great.'' Skirting the dance floor, he continued to usher her toward the front door. "Then we can leave?''

She shrugged in confusion. What had brought this on? "Sure.''

"Let's make tracks. Once we're back at your place we can regroup and decide where to go from here.''

Where to go? She knew where she should go—as far from Shayde as possible. Glancing at his set features she somehow doubted that would be possible. He had the look of a man on a mission. And she suspected *she* was that mission. The thought should have worried her. Instead, it filled her with warmth, initiating a gentle unraveling that caught her off guard. It took a few minutes to figure out where the emotions were coming from. Then it hit her.

She wasn't alone any longer.

In no time at all, Shayde plowed a steady course through clients, benefactors and co-workers, alike. He continued to amaze her with his ability to project a smooth graciousness combined with an unwavering determination in order to move them along the path he'd chosen. In no time they found themselves outside with the valet reluctantly turning over the keys to the Jag.

Tess regarded Shayde with amusement as he held the door for her. "I have to say, when you make up your mind to do something, you accomplish it in short order."

"Sorry. Did I rush you?"

"I didn't mind, if that's what you're asking. I was ready to leave before we even got there." A sudden thought occurred to her. "Would you mind if we swing by my office before you drop me at home? I have some files I need to pick up."

"Not at all. I'd also like to make a quick stop at my apartment, if that's okay."

"No problem."

Tess leaned back against the leather bucket seat and released her breath in a long sigh. Her hair had continued its downward trek to her shoulders and she pulled out the remaining clips, allowing the unruly curls to win the battle. Thank heavens the evening had finally ended. If she'd had to suffer through another hug or kiss or well-wisher, she'd have screamed. There had been far too many of them, despite Shayde's swift progress out of the door. The worst part was that every last one had been sincere.

The only good to come from their engagement would

be when Adelaide Smith learned of the engagement. Tess thought she'd caught a glimpse of the woman as they'd escaped out the door, but hadn't had an opportunity to find out for certain. Not that she could have handled a confrontation. She wasn't ready for Adelaide's discerning gaze to analyze her relationship with Shayde or to see the reality lurking beneath the Cinderella fantasy.

Tess glanced at Shayde. The lights from the dashboard flickered across his face, highlighting the sweeping planes and emphasizing every sharply carved angle in a startling contrast of light and dark. Nighttime suited him. Her mouth curved upward. So did the all-black tux he'd worn. What was it about this man that had convinced her to throw aside discretion and allow him to make love to her in such a public place? It defied comprehension.

"Don't worry, Tess." His silvery eyes flashed in her direction. "We'll work it out."

"You'll make sure of it?"

He shook his head. "*We'll* make sure of it. Despite what went down tonight, I'm not the type to ride roughshod over a woman and impose my wants on her."

"And if our wants coincide?" She couldn't believe she'd asked the question. What in the world had gotten into her?

"That's another story, isn't it?" His gaze landed on her again, hotter this time, full of masculine promise—and threat. "Do they coincide, sweetheart?"

She didn't dare answer that one. Calling herself every kind of coward, she closed her eyes. Maybe if she didn't look at him, she wouldn't be tempted to say something she shouldn't. To her relief, he allowed the conversation to lapse. They stopped briefly outside of a high-rise apartment building. With a murmured apology, Shayde disappeared inside. When he returned, he put the car in gear without explanation and continued on to Altruistics.

Tess unlocked the door to the office building with her key and checked in at the security desk. After a brief conversation with the chatty guard, they traversed the empty corridors in silence, their muffled footsteps bouncing eerily off the walls. Once in her office, she snapped on her desk lamp. The single circle of light eased across the black of the room. Beyond the narrow beam intense darkness surrounded them, forming a cage of shadows.

"I just need to pick up some files and then we can go," she murmured.

He stopped her before she could reach the file cabinet. "I have something for you first."

His voice sounded rougher than normal and she didn't understand why until she glanced at what he held. A small jeweler's box rested in the palm of his hand. Inside was the most gorgeous ring Tess had ever seen. Removing it from its velvet bed, he took her hand in his and slipped the ring on her finger.

"It's official now, sweetheart. You're mine."

CHAPTER SEVEN

TESS stared at the diamond ring in disbelief. It glittered like fire beneath the intense light flooding from her desk. The heavy gold band wrapped snugly about her finger, fitting as though made for her. Her hands trembled ever so slightly and shards of pink flashed from the heart of the oval solitaire. A pink diamond? She'd never seen anything like it before.

"Oh, Shayde," she whispered. "Is this why you stopped at your apartment? To pick up this ring?"

He nodded. "My grandfather brought the diamond over from Australia when he emigrated here. The stories are a bit vague as to how he got his hands on the stone in the first place, but his original plan was to sell it and start his own business. Instead, he gave it to my grandmother."

She looked up at him in dismay. "I can't accept this. You don't have to be an expert to know how rare these diamonds are. It must be worth a fortune. I'd be terrified of losing it."

"Consider it a temporary measure. You can return the ring when you don't need it any longer."

"No—"

She started to tug the diamond from her finger and he stopped her, closing his hand around hers with gentle insistence. "Your co-workers will expect you to show up at work tomorrow wearing an engagement ring. So will your clients."

113

Unexpected tears burned her eyes. "I can't. I can't wear your ring."

She felt his gaze on her, could sense him analyzing her reaction, weighing all the possibilities. "You're not betraying Robert," he finally said.

The air escaped her lungs in a soft sigh. How did he do it? Once again, he'd cut straight to the heart of the matter, hitting on what was bothering her with pinpoint accuracy. How did he manage to see so clearly all she kept hidden? It was an unnerving ability. It took a few seconds for her to regain her poise enough to respond. "You always amaze me when you do that."

He laughed, the sound husky with regret. "It only works if I keep an emotional distance. When I don't—" He shrugged. "You saw firsthand what happens when I get too close to a situation."

She couldn't resist teasing. "You pull a woman into the darkest corner and make passionate love to her?"

"Only every other Tuesday. And only with gorgeous redheads with pansy-blue eyes and a killer smile." He lifted her hand and studied the ring. "Did Robert give you a diamond? Is that why this is so hard for you?"

"No. We were pretty broke when we first married and decided the money could be put to better use. We bought simple gold bands instead." She fought to keep her voice steady. "Robert promised he'd give me a belated engagement ring when our first child was born, pick whichever gem was the baby's birthstone—"

The words caught in her throat and Shayde swore beneath his breath before wrapping her in a comforting embrace. "I'm so sorry, Tess. You loved him very much, didn't you?"

She nodded. "Six months wasn't nearly long enough."

"You still miss him."

He hadn't meant it as a question, but she answered, anyway. "Yes, though probably not in the way you mean." She rested her cheek against his chest and the steady thump of his heartbeat calmed her as she struggled to put her feelings into words. "I miss what we shared. I miss being with a man who understood me as thoroughly as I understood him. I miss… I miss the simple things like—" Her voice broke and she visibly fought for control. "Like being held like this. It's been ages since I've enjoyed something so basic. I'd forgotten how necessary it is."

His arms tightened around her. "All this time you've never found anyone who shares Robert's qualities?"

"Sure. Gray has them. He's quiet and thoughtful and has the same dry sense of humor. But I don't want another Robert." The confession escaped without volition. "He's part of my past."

The cadence of Shayde's breathing altered and she found herself glancing up at him, unable to look away. She shouldn't stare. She shouldn't sway closer. And she certainly shouldn't allow him to mold her into the sort of embrace they'd exchanged at the benefit.

"Maybe I can offer you something different for the future."

He whispered the words close to her lips. And then there was no more talking, just a collision of desire. He dug his hands into her hair, tilting her head to give him better access to her mouth. Surging inward, he mated his tongue with hers. It was a bold taking, edged with desperation. A blatant seduction. She responded in kind, needing all he had to offer.

She'd kept her distance from passion for too long. Fear kept her from acting—fear of loss, fear of betraying

Robert, fear that she could never feel for anyone else what she'd felt for him. What if she ended up experiencing a love as deep as the one that she'd known with her husband? What if it went deeper? What if she lost him the way she had Robert? In the back of her mind hovered the terror of living through those hideous dark days again.

With Shayde she risked all those possibilities. And yet she couldn't help herself. She'd been alone for too long, barren of emotional fulfillment for too many years. With one shattering kiss, she discovered that she wanted to live. She wanted a man in her life and in her bed. But most of all, she wanted him in her heart, to feel the depth and intensity and richness that comes when a woman commits to the man who completes her.

She didn't even realize she was crying until he broke the kiss, thumbing the tears from her cheeks. "Don't, Tess. Please don't cry. You don't have to wear the ring if you don't want to, not if it's going to upset you. We can tell people we haven't made a final selection, yet."

It didn't take any thought at all. "No." She might find the offer tempting, but the time had come to put the past behind her and look to the future. "I'll wear the ring."

"I didn't mean to make you cry."

She shook her head. "It wasn't your fault. You forced me to consider issues I'd been deliberately ignoring for these past few years." A sudden thought occurred to her, one that chased away the last of her tears. "You know… I just realized that I'm engaged to a man and I don't even know his last name."

He hesitated. "That's going to be a problem, isn't it?"

A wobbly smile tugged at her mouth. "Only if someone asks and I don't have an answer."

"We'll have to do something about that." To her exasperation, he shrugged the subject aside and she could tell from his expression that he'd already dismissed it as unimportant. "In the meantime, talk to me about these Impossibles you've been assigned."

"Ah." She nodded sagely. "A quick change of subject. Always an excellent way to duck an awkward question."

Amusement caused his eyes to gleam like starlight. "I already know Gray, so you don't have to give me any info about him."

She pretended to frown in deliberation. "And he knows you. Maybe I should ask him what your last name is."

"Excellent idea. You could say, 'Excuse me, Gray. Would you mind writing out a seven figure check, and while you're at it... What's my fiancé's surname?'"

"You think he might find it strange?" She sighed in mock regret. "Oh, well. It was a thought."

"Tell me about Walt Moore."

She held up her hand, sparkling flashes of pink emphasizing the sweeping movement. "Hold the presses. You mean there's someone out there you haven't met? I'm shocked. You seem to know everyone else." Her eyes narrowed in speculation. "Now that I think about it, you *do* know a lot of people. Bull. Seth. Gray. You run in some interesting circles."

"Walt. Moore. Talk."

She gave in to his request. Request? Hah! More like a demand. "In a nutshell, Mr. Moore is an older gentleman of sour disposition and a hermitlike existence who has the reputation of a modern day Scrooge."

"Charming. Any chance we can take a page out of

Dickens' book and arrange a visitation from a trio of cooperative ghosts?''

"Unlikely." She shot him an inquisitive look. "Unless you're on intimate terms with any? As I mentioned, you seem to know most everyone else, why not ghosts?"

"Sorry. The spirits of Christmas past, present and future haven't crossed paths with me to date. But the minute they do, I'll drop them a warning about Moore." He watched as she removed the pertinent files from a nearby metal cabinet and deposited them on the desk beside him. He nudged the top file. "How about Dick Smith? What's his story?"

"I don't know him. My understanding is that he prefers to stay out of the limelight, unlike his mother."

"Okay, now you've got me." Dismissing the files, he leaned against her desk, regarding her intently. "I could have sworn you reacted when Portman assigned him to you. Is he the one putting the moves on you or isn't he?"

"He's not." She waited a beat and then admitted, "His mother is."

"Adelaide is interested in you?" Shayde asked politely.

She stared in amazement. "This just gets better and better. You know Adelaide, too?"

"Far too well."

"Then you should know what an inveterate matchmaker she is."

"Considering she's spent the better part of the last ten years trying to marry me off to anyone who even vaguely qualifies as female?" His mouth tightened carving deep furrows in each cheek. "Yes, I'm familiar with that less than stellar quality."

"Adelaide is trying to set me up with her son."

"Which son?"

"*Which* son?" Tess sank into the chair behind her desk. "You have got to be kidding me. You mean there's more than one? Oh, I don't think I can handle this. You're telling me that if she fails with the first—"

"That would be Tom."

"Tom?" Tess's brows pulled together. "She didn't mention that one."

"Then there's Dick. I gather she skipped directly to him?"

"Tom and Dick Smith?" Tess was torn between laughter and horror. "No! Tell me there's not a Harry."

He grinned. "There is. But you won't need to worry about Adelaide setting you up with her youngest."

"Already married?"

"No. Harry's a girl, poor thing."

Tess could only stare, appalled. "How could Adelaide have named her children Tom, Dick and Harry? Does she hate them?"

"She has a— I guess you could call it a unique sense of humor. She once told me she picked those particular names so she wouldn't have trouble remembering them." His expression grew contemplative. "I think I believed her for all of two minutes before the twinkle in her eye gave her away."

"Her poor children."

"She's actually a wonderful woman. Just—"

"Unique."

"Exactly." A frown lined Shayde's brow. "Are you telling me that Adelaide is the reason you hired me?"

"Yes."

"Incredible." He shook his head in disgust. "You can't handle one crazy woman's matchmaking schemes without going to these extremes?"

He'd put her on the defensive and Tess escaped from her chair, stepping outside the circle of light. The heavy shadows reached out and wrapped tight around her, veiling her from Shayde's keen gaze. "For your information, I've been handling them for five years. And I'd have kept handling them if it hadn't been for an unfortunate complication."

He didn't shift from his position, but continued to lean against her desk. The light gilded the darkness of his hair and tux and turned his eyes to pure silver. "Let me guess. Dick Smith runs smack into your promotion."

"Exactly. After failing to spark a romance between me and the various men she's deemed worthy, Adelaide took it into her head that her son and I would make the perfect couple and nothing I said would change her mind."

"Why didn't you just meet the guy and blow him off?"

"You already hit on it. The promotion. About the same time all this happened with Adelaide, Al began dropping heavy hints that her son was the Impossible I was expected to turn in order to get my promotion."

"And?"

Didn't he understand? "And it's a conflict of interest."

Shayde shrugged, the easy movement pulling his tux taut across an impressive set of shoulders. It annoyed her that she'd notice such a thing when there were far more imperative concerns deserving her attention. It annoyed her even more that he was so oblivious to the impact he had on her. Maybe if he knew how badly he distracted her, he'd...

She bit back an exclamation of annoyance. He'd what? Shrink his shoulders? Turn his eyes from an intriguing shade of quicksilver to something more non-descript? Dilute the power of his masculinity? Yeah, right. No doubt he'd hop on those suggestions. Thank goodness she stood in darkness and he couldn't see her reaction to him. It was a small saving grace, but the only thing that kept her from total humiliation.

"Come on, Tess. Be reasonable." To her relief, he seemed oblivious to her wayward thoughts. "So you go out with the guy. You laugh about how awkward it all is because his mother is sweet and romantic, not to mention nutty as a fruitcake. And then you hit him up for a couple mill."

"And then?" she demanded. "What happens when we land on my doorstep and he wants me to show my appreciation for those couple mill?"

"Simple. You duck his kiss, stick out your hand and tell him it's a pleasure doing business with him and anytime he's in the neighborhood, feel free to drop off another check." He lifted an eyebrow. "What's so tough about that?

"Cute, but it doesn't work that way. This is a serious business."

"I realize that."

"No, I don't think you do." The light drew her from the shadows. Or was it the man standing within the light's embrace? "We're talking about donors who contribute thousands upon thousands of dollars to causes that could mean the difference between life and death to countless people. We're constantly scrutinized for the least impropriety, both in the way we handle the money that comes in and the way we go about soliciting it. I can't have a personal relationship with a donor. I don't solicit funds that way."

"Dammit, Tess. I didn't mean to suggest—"

"But other people will," she cut in. "That's why I went to the extreme of hiring you. If I'm already involved in a serious relationship, any dealings with Adelaide's son will be seen as strictly professional. I can approach him, explain all the ways in which his donation will benefit the causes we support. If he says no, someone else will take another crack at him at some point in the future. And if he says yes, I'll have won the promotion through sheer hard work."

"Death before dishonor," he murmured wryly. "Is that it?"

"More like, no job promotion unless it's achieved on the up-and-up."

"So what now?"

"Now I go through the files on the three Impossibles and see if they contain any information that'll help me determine an avenue of approach."

Shayde straightened, nodding decisively. "In that case, I'll take you home so you can get to work."

"Thank you." She owed him more than a simple thank you. Far more. "I also appreciate how you covered for me tonight. You didn't have to tell Al we were engaged. I know you were trying to protect me, and you were right when you said announcing our engagement was the only way out of a sticky situation. If you hadn't come up with a reasonable explanation, Al would have—"

"Forget it," he cut her off brusquely. "Everything worked out in the end. Just as our engagement will eventually work out, too."

She couldn't help but marvel. "You sound so confident."

"That's because I am." He picked up the files she'd removed from the cabinet. "Ready to go?"

"Considering how long a night I have ahead of me, I guess we'd better."

They left her office and signed out at the security desk, bidding the guard a friendly goodnight. Shayde's Jag sat all alone in the employee parking lot, prompting a moment's idle speculation. So much about him didn't add up—the car, the ring, his familiarity with so many of Altruistics' benefactors. There was a mystery here and the minute she had some free time she intended to solve it.

"Don't let it bother you," he murmured, reading her mind again.

"Oh, I won't." She smiled complacently. "I'll figure it out soon enough and then it won't bother me at all."

The drive home didn't take long, mainly because they didn't get held up at any of the draw bridges that made Seattle such a distinctive place to live. "Would you like some help going through those files?" Shayde asked as they pulled up outside of her Green Lake house.

"No, thanks." She yawned. "I can handle it."

"I don't doubt that for a minute. I just thought the two of us together could accomplish more than one alone. And we could probably do it a lot faster, too." He smiled at her frown. "Would you reconsider if I promise this isn't an excuse to seduce you?"

"I should have known you wouldn't try something that obvious."

He chuckled softly. "Sure I would." He tucked a lock of hair behind her ear, his thumb leaving a scorching trail along the curve of her cheek. "But not tonight. Not with something this important."

She could feel herself wavering between the possibility that his knowledge of Grayson Shaw and the Smiths would benefit her research, and a more basic and far less noble need for his company. "Do you really think you can help?"

"I wouldn't offer if I didn't think so."

She nodded, giving in to a desire she was too tired to resist. "All right. Come on in. Maybe between the two of us we can get through those files before sunup."

Once inside, Tess changed into jeans and an oversize shirt that not only covered every inch of skin between shoulder and waist, but practically hung to her knees. Next, she rolled up her sleeves and put on a pot of coffee in preparation for the hours of work they had ahead of them. Carrying the mugs into the den, she found Shayde waiting for her.

He'd removed his tux jacket, tossed aside his cummerbund and bow tie, and yanked free the first few studs of his dress shirt. Stripped of his civilized veneer, he looked dark and dangerous and entirely too attractive. He sat on the edge of the couch, the three files spread across the coffee table in front of him. Oh, no. *The couch.* She stumbled to a halt, unable to help remembering what had happened the last time they'd shared that particular piece of furniture. Had it only been last night? Incredible.

"Hand me the coffee and try not to think about it," he said absently as he flipped through the files.

"Excuse me?"

"You were remembering last night. And I was telling you—"

"Not to think about it. Got it." She passed him one of the mugs and lied in her most cheerful tone of voice. "Not a problem."

"I wish I could say the same." He shot her a glance every bit as scalding as the coffee. "But I made you a

promise and come hell or high water, I intend to keep
it.''

''In that case, maybe the couch isn't such a good
idea.''

''It's a great idea.'' His gaze over the rim of the mug
turned wicked. ''Just not for what we have in mind for
tonight's activities.''

She closed her eyes, hoping that once temptation was
out of sight, it would also be out of mind. ''What did
you say about keeping your promise? Something about
come hell or high water?''

''Relax. I'm done teasing.'' He took a quick swallow
of coffee and selected one of the files, dropping it on
top of the others. Just like that he switched from charming seducer to serious businessman. ''Let's start with
Gray.''

She forced herself to follow Shayde's lead and focus
on work. ''Why him?''

''Because he lives in San Francisco, not Seattle, which
means he won't be in town for long. The other two are
local. You can approach them at your convenience. But
you'll only have access to Gray for a limited time.''

''I'll tell you what. Let's do a general overview of
each candidate and then we'll discuss them one at a time
and dig a little deeper.'' She pulled a notepad and pen
from her briefcase. Flipping to the first page, she made
a few notations. ''First up, Grayson Shaw. I've approached him on three separate occasions so far and
though he's always polite, nothing I've said about
Altruistics has made an impression.''

''Gray's very logical. He's also not easily swayed by
emotion. So make sure any dealings you have with him
address the nuts and bolts of the situation.'' Shayde
thumped a finger against one of the pages. ''Something

you might want to add to your file is that Gray's favorite restaurant in Seattle is House Milano.''

She lifted an eyebrow. "Taking him to his favorite restaurant is supposed to turn him? I thought you said he was logical.''

"Hey, what's more logical than appealing to the man's stomach?''

"The food's that good?''

"Honey, if you hand Gray a list of all the good causes Altruistics benefits, and combine it with you, the view from House Milano, and Joe Milano's food, I don't see how you can lose. If all that doesn't convince Gray to fork over his money, nothing will.''

She stirred uneasily. Why throw her into the mix? "But you'll be with me, right? I don't want him to get the wrong idea.''

Shayde hesitated. "Sure. No problem.''

She flipped open the next file. "Okay. Tell me about Dick Smith. What's he like?''

"A total idiot.''

She grimaced. "That bad, huh?''

Shayde leaned back against the couch cushions and stretched. "I used to think he was an okay sort of guy. But now I'm not so sure.''

"Okay, explain why.''

He snorted. "Any man who lets his mommy pick his women for him has to be an idiot.''

"Really?'' Tess regarded Shayde in amusement. "Considering I'm the woman Adelaide selected, I'm not sure whether to be flattered or insulted.''

"That only makes him more of an idiot. Either he should have realized a hell of a lot sooner what phenomenally good taste Mommy has, or he should have found you without her help.''

"Got it. The poor man can't win in your book."

"Not a chance."

The next couple of hours flew by. Tess discovered that Shayde was an invaluable source of information. When they'd first met, he'd told her he had an instinct for reading people, that he saw beneath the surface. He proved it in the short time they worked together. She found his insight staggering as he analyzed the situation and offered suggestions on how best to approach each man. If she hadn't been so exhausted or so concerned about keeping their conversation out of the realm of the personal, she'd have asked how a man of Shayde's obvious talents ended up working for a temp agency.

They kept at it until the hands on the clock crept well past midnight. Checking his watch, Shayde stood. "Why don't I brew up a fresh pot of coffee?" he offered. "Another hour and I think we'll have done all the prep work possible. I assume the next step will be to arrange an initial meeting with everyone?"

Tess nodded absently, running her hands through her hair. "Coffee. Good." The curls tumbled back into her face in utter disobedience and Shayde couldn't help smiling. Even exhausted and totally focused on work, she looked gorgeous. Ruffling the rebellious curls, he headed for the kitchen. Five minutes later, he returned and found Tess slumped to one side on the couch, sound asleep.

"Okay. Maybe we'll stop now. What do you say to that, boss lady?" He waited for a response he knew full well wouldn't come. "You agree? Perfect. Time for bed."

Setting the mugs aside, he gently lifted her into his arms. She felt good. Too good. Worse, she felt like she belonged. She stirred, her lashes fluttering against her pale cheeks. Aside from heaving a gusty sigh she didn't wake, much to his relief. He didn't think she'd appreciate any explanation he might offer as to how she'd ended up in his arms, no matter how noble his intentions.

It didn't take long to track down her bedroom. Opening the most likely door, he looked around and grinned. So. He'd been right. Her inner sanctum was decorated in bold, striking colors, the interior as bright and radiant as a jeweled butterfly. He deposited her on the bed and removed her shoes. Standing there for a moment, he debated how much further to strip her. With a fatalistic shrug, he slid his hands beneath her voluminous shirt and unsnapped her jeans. Tugging them downward, he folded them across a nearby chair. Finally, he tucked her beneath the covers.

It was time to leave. It was also time to take care of one other unpleasant duty. "We both have a job to do, don't we, sweetheart?" he murmured regretfully. "I guess we'd better get those jobs done, no matter how resistant we are to the idea." Leaning down, he took her mouth in a kiss as gentle as it was hungry. "Goodbye, Tess. Sweet dreams."

After collecting his belongings, Shayde left her house, locking the doors behind him. The minute he walked outside, he flipped open his cell phone. He'd better tell Shadoe how badly he'd screwed up before his brother heard it from another source. He'd also better not let on the intense masculine satisfaction that screwup afforded him. Then he'd have to get to work. Whether he liked the idea or not, he couldn't duck his responsibilities any longer.

The time had come to instigate a romance between Tess and Gray.

CHAPTER EIGHT

"WHAT'S the status?" Shadoe's boss demanded.

He hung up the phone. "Oh, my brother is making an excellent hash out of the entire assignment."

"Explain."

"He's botching it, lady."

"You have to correct it."

"No, not, yet." Leaning back in his chair, Shadoe folded his hands behind his head and propped his feet on the desk. "I have every confidence in my little brother. He'll get it straightened out in time."

"And if he fails?"

"Shayde fail?" Shadoe pondered the concept. "What's the chance of that?"

"I've checked my math twice," she fussed. "It keeps coming up as ten to one in favor of his failing."

"Really? Are you certain?" He frowned. "I had the odds of success calculated as much better than that."

"No. Ten to one against."

"Ten to one," Shadoe repeated. He smiled complacently. "How very encouraging. As skilled as he is, I was afraid he might actually pull it off."

The instant Shayde ended the call with Shadoe, he punched in another number. The phone was answered on the first ring.

"Yes, dear?"

"Mother? What the *hell* have you done?"

129

"Dick, darling. Do you have any idea what time it is?"

"Don't 'Dick, darling' me. I want an explanation and I want it now."

"It's two in the morning." She paused a beat. "Now that we've settled that, are you going to tell me about what I'm supposed to explain or is this a guessing game?"

"You want a guessing game? I have two words for you, Mother. Tess Lonigan."

"Darling girl. So sad how she lost her husband. I've done my best to help." Adelaide heaved a sigh. "But she's a wee bit stubborn."

"Then you admit it? You've been matchmaking again."

"Of course," she answered promptly. "You know it gives me something to do."

Shayde gritted his teeth. "You need to stop and stop now."

"Done. In fact, you didn't even have to ask. Wasn't that easy?" She didn't wait for his response. "Besides... It's all been taken care of."

"What does that mean?"

"It means that I'm finished with Tess."

Hell. "And what does *that* mean?"

"Since she's found the perfect husband, my job is done. Oh, and by the way, congratulations on your engagement, dear. I couldn't have done better if I'd chosen her for you myself. Oh, wait." Her laughter came through loud and clear. "I did choose her for you, didn't I? Have a lovely evening."

The connection went dead and Shayde snapped his phone closed, dropping it in his pocket. He should have known that Adelaide would be one step ahead of him.

He shook his head in disgust. His mother was always one step ahead of her children. Okay, fine. So, Adelaide knew what he'd done. That couldn't be helped. Right now he had to decide on his next move. His mouth tightened. He knew what that move would have to be. He'd do what he'd promised. He'd make sure Tess received her happily-ever-after ending.

Even if it meant that he wouldn't.

Toward dawn Tess awoke from the strangest dream. She'd been in her den, stretched out on the couch working a jigsaw puzzle she'd spread across the coffee table. Shayde sat beside her and every time she reached for a certain piece, he'd take it away.

"Not that one," he'd murmur.

She tried every other piece in that particular hole, but none of them worked. Finally, she took the piece away from Shayde and slipped it into the space. It fit perfectly.

"Oops." He grinned at her. "Caught me."

Tess released her breath in a long sigh, the remnants of the dream fading. Gazing up at the ceiling she yawned. "Yup. I caught you. Now the question is… What do I do with you?"

As Shayde's first order of business, he filled Tess's office with flowers. It didn't further his assignment to instigate a romance with Gray, but he couldn't help thinking that every newly engaged woman should have her office filled with flowers from a lovesick fiancé.

Next came a duty he didn't look forward to. But he had a job to accomplish, and he'd get it done, regardless of how he might feel about it personally…and personally he'd come to despise what he'd been assigned to do. Picturing Tess in Gray's arms—imagining her responding to another man's kisses the way she'd responded to his, thinking about someone else touching her as intimately as he'd touched her—stirred something dark and elemental. He didn't understand the possessiveness that gripped him. Or perhaps he was afraid to examine it too closely for fear of what he'd discover about himself.

Whatever the cause, it required every scrap of willpower for Shayde to pick up the phone and place a call to Gray.

The call might have been a mistake.

In less than an hour, Tess stood outside his apartment door, hammering away with unmistakable fury. Even her hair underscored her outrage. The vibrant curls escaped her slicked back style and bounced around her face, punctuating every movement in a colorful swirl of chaotic abandon. He didn't dare ask how she'd managed to talk her way past the security desk. Even more unnerving was how she'd found his apartment when she didn't even know his name.

The instant he opened the door, she swept across his threshold, bristling from stem to stern like an orange tabby whose fur had been brushed the wrong way. "Start talking, Shayde. I want to hear exactly what you said to Gray and why." Three steps in and she stopped dead, gazing around wide-eyed. "Oh, wow."

"Please." He slammed the door shut behind her. "Come in."

She took a full minute to examine what she could of his apartment from where she stood in the foyer, even standing on tippytoes to catch a glimpse of the living area. "This place is *incredible*. I mean really… incredible." With a reluctant sigh, she turned to face him, her attention switching to the matter that had brought her banging on his door. Renewed anger swiftly overrode curiosity. "Okay. Talk."

"I don't suppose you'd care to go back to incredible?"

She waved the red herring aside without so much as a nibble. "We'll get to that soon enough. First I want to know precisely what you said to Gray and why."

"Me?" Shayde feigned innocence, something he didn't do very well. With a bit of luck she might not notice, though considering Tess's powers of perception, it was a long shot at best. "What are you talking about?"

"You told Grayson Shaw how our engagement came about."

Aw, hell. Next time he saw his good ol' buddy, Gray, he'd get some payback. A solid poke in the nose wouldn't go amiss. Shayde scowled. Now that he thought about it, maybe he'd be really generous and give his indiscreet friend a second one, just to make certain the lesson took. "Oh. That."

"Yes. That." He caught a note in her voice that left him wincing. "How could you? How could you tell him something so private?"

Hurt appeared to be her overriding emotion and it bothered him more than he cared to admit that he was responsible for causing that hurt. He grappled for an excuse—anything—that would set their relationship right again. "Look, sweetheart, he tricked it out of me." Okay, lame. But desperation did pitiful things to a man.

"Tricked it out of you? You. Tricked." Tess must have found the excuse lame, as well. She stared at him with such patent disbelief that it took every ounce of self-possession not to scuff the toe of his shoe like some sort of callow schoolboy. How the hell did she do it? "Now there's an oxymoron if I ever heard one."

He cleared his throat. "Blame it on a late night and not enough coffee this morning."

"Stop the games, Shayde." Hurt turned to irritation. "It's not like you. With one exception, you've always been aboveboard in your dealings with me."

One exception? Maybe he'd be better off not asking which exception she meant, considering he could call to mind at least two separate occasions in which he'd been less than totally frank. But since honesty was such a vital issue with her—and usually with him, for that matter—he'd take a wild stab at an "aboveboard" response.

"Our engagement was my fault, so I told Gray the truth about what happened. I hoped by warning him in advance that he wouldn't blame you when we ended our relationship. I didn't want there to be any question in his mind about where the responsibility fell."

His explanation went a long way toward mollifying her. "I should warn you that whatever you told Gray upset him. For some reason he was very concerned about my well-being."

"Good. I'm glad he's concerned about you." Good? If it was so good, why did Shayde have an overwhelming urge to throw something? He should be delighted that Gray's protective impulses had kicked in with Tess, instead of reacting like a bull catching the scent of a rival. "You must be pleased he was comfortable enough to call. It puts you on a much friendlier footing. That should prove helpful when you approach him for a donation, right?" If his observation held a savage edge, it couldn't be helped. He felt a bit savage around the edges.

"No, it's not helpful and I'm not in the least comfortable about being on a friendlier footing with Gray.

I'm trying to maintain a professional distance here, remember?'' She scrutinized him in a way that had every internal warning system going to red alert. "I wonder what he knows about you that has him so concerned. I don't suppose you have any idea?''

"None.'' Time to change the subject and fast. "Look, if it makes you feel better, something positive came out of our phone call.'' He didn't wait for her to ask. Better to keep the conversation moving along. "I used my most clever maneuvers and crafty finagling to get my hands on Gray's schedule for the next few days.''

To his satisfaction she looked impressed, the last of her anger dying away. "How did you manage to pull that off?''

He grinned. "I asked him.''

She stared for a split second, then her mouth twitched and she broke down and laughed. "You're too clever for me, Shayde. I never would have thought of that option.''

Her laughter helped ease his tension, soothing some of the primitive urges he'd been fighting ever since they'd first met and enabling him to respond with deceptive lightness. "That's why you hired me, because I'm the best.'' Unable to keep his hands off her, he tucked a wayward curl into place. "Gray told me he's free for lunch on Friday. I booked a table at Milano's for one o'clock. All you have to do is extend the invitation.''

"What?'' she teased. "You didn't take care of that detail, too?''

He shrugged. He'd laid the preliminary groundwork to instigate a romance between Tess and Gray. Did he have to serve the woman up on a platter, too? Not a chance in hell. "Hey, it's your promotion. I know how important it is that you earn it on your own."

"And I will."

He smiled tenderly. "I don't doubt that for a minute." He gestured in the direction of the kitchen. "Can I get you a cup of coffee?"

"No, thanks. I'm still floating in coffee from last night." A frown touched her brow and Shayde released his breath in a silent sigh. He could guess what their next topic of discussion would entail. Sure enough, she glanced at him, a hint of pink riding high on her cheekbones. "Speaking of last night…"

His jaw inched out defensively. "Yes, I carried you to your room. And yes, I removed your shoes."

"What about my jeans?"

If his jaw poked out any further he'd dislocate it. "They sort of fell off."

"Fell off." She nodded sagely. "Got it."

Perhaps a bit of embellishing was in order. "I guess they don't make jeans the way they used to. Fall asleep and look what happens."

"And did my jeans also fold themselves across my chair?"

"Technology today." He shook his head in amazement. "Self-folding jeans. What's next?"

"Shayde—"

Just like that the tenor of the conversation changed. The easy banter faded, replaced by something that sharpened the air, a longing that felt both hot and desperate. He couldn't say what kept him from pulling her into his arms. Perhaps he still possessed some lingering trace of honor or sense of fair play that prevented him from acting. More than anything he wanted to kiss her until they completed what had begun the first moment he walked into her office and met her wary gaze. But instead of giving in to the baser side of his nature, he closed his hands into fists and kept his feet planted where they were, fighting the overwhelming impetus to make her his own.

"I didn't peek." All that he couldn't say burned in his eyes. "But I wanted to. I carried you to your bedroom and saw the inner sanctum. I undressed you as far as I dared. And then I left."

"Are you always so noble?"

It was the wrong thing to ask. He wasn't the least noble. Lurking beneath the civilized veneer existed feelings that stripped him of all control, that reduced him to the most primitive of urges. He wanted Tess. The compulsion was so strong he could barely contain it. A desperate need coalesced into a single imperative—the drive to take what instinct told him was his. This woman belonged to him, just as he belonged to her. He didn't understand how he knew. He didn't have a hope in hell of putting a socially acceptable label on those feelings. He simply accepted the gut-level certainty that without Tess, his life was wrong.

"Dammit, Tess! Don't you get it?" he demanded. "I didn't want to be noble. I wanted to strip you down to nothing and make you mine in every sense of the word. I wanted that engagement ring on your finger to be real."

The oddest expression swept across her face. It couldn't be longing. Not for him. They weren't meant for each other. "But it isn't real."

"No, it's not. And you were vulnerable last night. I couldn't take advantage of you under those circumstances."

It was her turn to offer a tender smile. "You couldn't take advantage of me under any circumstances."

His mouth twisted. "Don't be so sure. You don't know me, Tess. There's a lot I haven't told you."

"Care to fill me in now?" she asked gently.

He didn't dare. It would ruin their relationship, not to mention preventing him from completing his job. He couldn't bring himself to do that. But her question—and the potential ramifications of that question—firmed his resolve. "I think we'd be wise to finish our respective jobs. You have an Impossible to turn. And I—"

"And you...what?" She studied him with open curiosity. "What do you have to do, Shayde?"

"I have to help you." He said it for his own benefit as much as for hers. "And making love to you won't help."

She actually had the nerve to pat his arm. "Don't feel bad," she deadpanned. "You can't be good at everything."

Hell. "Honey, don't tempt me to prove you wrong." He pushed the words out through tightly clamped teeth. "Trust me, it would be a true pleasure."

Temptation sparked in her gaze, as well as that strange longing that he'd caught earlier. "I wish—"

He shook his head. "Don't say it."

She released a soft sigh. "Okay. I won't. But you can't stop me from thinking it."

Or stop himself, for that matter. He swore beneath his breath. What a mess. How could instigating one simple romance have gone so horribly wrong? And how did he fix it when every fiber of his being urged him to make this woman his before she was taken from him. He draped an arm around her shoulders and opened the door to his apartment.

"Come on. Let's get out of here before I do something we'll both regret."

She leaned into his hold. "Now that's scary," she murmured.

"What?"

She shot him a scorching look. "That was exactly what I was going to say."

Okay, so he'd promised himself he wouldn't show up at the luncheon appointment. He'd sworn up one side and down the other that he'd give Gray a fair shot at Tess. Shayde checked his watch. An hour could be considered a fair shot, right? And if not… His jaw tightened. Tough. He'd waited as long as he could. After all, he was the Instigator. Checking on the development of the romance topped his job description which meant that dropping by House Milano to see how the two of them were getting along fell strictly under the heading of "in the line of duty."

He kept up the argument during the entire elevator ride to the restaurant crowning King Tower. Stepping into the marble-floored lobby, he greeted the elderly maître d' with a broad smile. "How's it going, Georgio?"

"Excellent, Mr.—"

"Shayde," he interrupted hastily. Damn. It was a good thing he hadn't crashed the party when Tess and Gray had first arrived. His cover would have been blown, for sure, and no doubt his adorable employer would have taken him apart piece by painful piece. "It's Shayde today."

"Certainly, sir."

Before he could ask about Tess, Gray walked into the lobby from the direction of the main dining area.

Catching sight of Shayde, he scowled. "Okay, *friend*. What the hell's going on?"

An irrational anger gripped Shayde. He vaguely recalled owing Gray something. Something to do with Tess— Oh, yeah. A fierce grin split his face. He owed his ol' buddy a poke in the nose. And he was in the perfect mood to dole it out. "Having a good lunch?" he practically snarled.

Whether it was his tone or the fact that he'd bunched himself like a tiger about to pounce, he couldn't say. But one of the two incited Gray to react. In two bounds the two men collided, crashing against the nearest wall.

"Why are you throwing your fiancée in my face at every opportunity?" Gray demanded.

Shayde grabbed his former friend by the throat. "Did you touch her? I swear, if you did—"

"Sure I touched her." Gray's blue eyes turned to flame and he bunched his fists around Shayde's lapels. "The phrase 'would you like some sugar' took on a whole new meaning. We rocked House Milano like it's never been rocked before."

Before Shayde could do more than grit out a single expletive, Georgio appeared at their side. "Gentlemen." His calmly accented tones washed over them like ice water. "Do not force me to expel two of House Milano's favorite customers as though you were no better than unruly schoolboys."

For an endless minute the two men locked gazes. Slowly, reluctantly, they released each other. "I apologize, Georgio," Shayde muttered. "I don't know what got into me."

Georgio's expression turned indulgent. "Redheads were always one of my weaknesses, as well," he commented. "But I believe you'll find that isn't the case with Mr. Shaw.'' With a final warning look, the maître d' returned to his stance behind the reservation desk.

Gray shook his head, an amused expression supplanted his anger. "He's right you know. Tess is drop-dead gorgeous, but she's not my type. Which brings us to an interesting question..." His gaze grew uncomfortably analytical. "Why have you been throwing her at me this past week? If you want me to donate to Altruistics, just ask me.''

"Okay, fine. How about making a donation?''

"Done.''

"Great." Shayde thrust a hand through his hair. He'd never felt so awkward before in his life. So much for being the smooth-as-silk Instigator, gliding behind the scenes and setting romance into motion. "Would it help any if I reminded you she's not really my fiancée?''

"Not even a little. Now, give. What's going on?''

Shayde released his breath in a sigh. "Not interested, huh?''

"If there weren't someone else, I would have been tempted. But no, I'm not interested." He thumped a finger against Shayde's chest. "And if I felt toward a woman the way you clearly feel toward your non-fiancée, I'd stop making such an ass out of myself and find a way to turn fantasy into reality.''

Shayde grimaced. Now why hadn't he thought of that? "Then you're out of the picture?''

"I was never in the picture. Tell Tess I'll have my people cut her a check first thing next week." Gray inclined his head in the direction of the archway leading into the main section of the restaurant. "She's waiting for you, by the way. I told her you wouldn't show, but apparently you promised you would and that settled the issue as far as she's concerned. That's a lot of faith wrapped up in one woman. I suggest you do everything you can not to destroy it.''

"I haven't lied to her." Not exactly.

"You think she'll see it the same way?" Gray didn't give him time to reply. "Fair warning, Shayde. She's mad as hell. Not that I blame her. Try coming clean. Who knows? It might work."

With that he stepped into an elevator that had just disgorged a carful of customers, leaving Shayde to stare after him. So much for the Committee's perfect match. What the hell were they thinking? The man didn't want her. Of course, that meant Gray must be insane. No doubt it wasn't something the Committee had taken into consideration when they'd picked him.

Shayde followed the pathway of pink and ivory marble across the lobby and entered the restaurant in search of Tess. He spotted her at a table near the windows. As Gray had warned, she looked annoyed. Temper had given her cheeks a rosy flush and turned her eyes a darker shade of blue. Even her hair looked more fiery than usual. The minute she spotted him, she reached for her glass and took a healthy swig of wine.

Uh-oh.

What had Gray told her? It couldn't have been much. If she knew everything, he doubted she'd still be sitting there. He reached the table and stood by the chair across from her. More than anything he wanted to gather her in his arms and give her all the sugar she'd ever need and to hell with the Committee. Not that she'd appreciate the offer. One glance warned that she'd focused her full attention on business.

He fought for restraint, donning his most professional mask. "Should I sit?"

"Only if you want to hang onto your job."

He pulled out the chair. Okay. So far, so good. "Sorry I'm late."

"Me, too. I've just sat through one of the most embarrassing lunches I've ever had the misfortune of experiencing."

He shouldn't ask, but he suspected it didn't really matter. He was going to hear about it whether he prompted the explanation or not. "Embarrassing?" he inquired politely. "How so?"

"Can the innocence, Shayde. It isn't going to work." She folded her hands in a neat little pile and compressed her mouth in a way that had him dying to ease it with a slow, deep kiss. "Just how well do you know Gray?"

He met her gaze squarely and pushed all thoughts of kissing her from his thoughts. He couldn't afford the distraction right now. He'd hoped she wouldn't discover the truth about his friendship with Gray until after she'd won her promotion. But he'd been prepared for the issue to come up at some point. "I know him well enough."

His confession didn't please her. "*How* well?"

No way was he going to get out of this one. "We were college roommates," he admitted.

If he thought she looked annoyed before, it was nothing compared to how she looked now. Her pile of fingers squeezed into a white-knuckle grip and her lips compacted so tightly it would take one hell of a kiss to pry them apart again. "And you didn't see fit to mention that minor detail before?" Somehow the words escaped her mouth, though he couldn't quite figure out how.

"I thought about it and decided it wouldn't be a good idea."

"And why not?"

"Because you'd have crossed Gray off your list."

That stopped her. "What do you mean?" she demanded.

"I mean that if you knew I was in a position to put pressure on the guy, you'd have refused to try and turn him. And why?" He shrugged. "Conflict of interest, of course. Same as with Adelaide."

"It was my decision to make," she argued.

"You're kidding, right?" He sprawled backward in the chair, regarding her in frustration. "I knew what decision you'd make. Hell, sweetheart, you hired me at the mere suggestion of a *potential* conflict with Dick Smith. What do you call this if not a conflict of interest?"

"You're right. It *is* a conflict of interest, one I should have been told about."

"Okay, fine. Now you know. Are you going to solicit a donation from Gray, or not?"

Sure enough, she shook her head. "I'm not."

"Why?" Not that he needed to ask. He already knew the answer.

"Because he was your college roommate. He'll feel obligated to contribute something and I won't gain my promotion that way."

"Your *promotion?*" He felt his own temper rising to match hers and he leaned across the table toward her. "What about the benefit to Altruistics? Do you think they care where the money comes from or whether Gray writes a check because he's an old friend of your fiancé's? I guarantee, they won't. The check will get cashed either way and the money will help a slew of excellent causes."

"You don't understand." She leaned forward, too, until their noses came within inches of each other. "I *have* to get this promotion through my own efforts. I can't accept outside help."

"Why?" he repeated, more urgently this time. "And why is how you get those donations more important than getting your hands on the money? Doesn't the good it'll provide outweigh every other consideration?"

She opened her mouth, before closing it again. The fight drained out of her and she released her breath in a long sigh. "I'm overreacting, aren't I?"

His anger faded and he leaned forward, covering her hand with his. "What's going on, Tess? You're taking this whole death before dishonor thing to an extreme. I don't understand any of it."

"Shayde—" She stopped, unable to continue.

"Talk to me, sweetheart," he insisted gently. "Why is this so important to you?"

She started to reply, but the words caught in her throat. To his concern, tears welled up in her eyes.

Shayde didn't hesitate. "Has the bill been taken care of?" At her frantic nod, he tossed down a few extra bills to cover their holding the table for so long and shoved back his chair. "Let's get out of here."

Wrapping an arm around her, he escorted her from the restaurant. Passing Georgio, he signaled the elderly man that everything was under control and stabbed the button for the elevator. In a few short minutes they were transported from the top of King Tower to the parking garage beneath, and thirty seconds after that Shayde had Tess ensconced in the passenger seat of his Jag.

Pulling his cell phone from his pocket, he tossed it onto her lap. "Call your office and tell them you'll be unavailable for the rest of the day." To his relief, she didn't argue, but placed the call. "My place or yours?" he asked the second she was done.

"I think I could use a dose of incredible right now," she confessed.

Shayde nodded. "My place."

They completed the drive in total silence. He spared Tess a single glance and then didn't look her way again. He couldn't, not if they were going to get to his apartment without stopping. She appeared utterly defeated and it was everything he could do to keep the car on the road instead of pulling into the nearest parking lot and demanding an explanation.

It took forever to park his car, ring for the elevator and endure the endless ride to his floor. The instant they walked into his apartment, he slammed the door closed and wrapped his arms around her. He held her without speaking for a long minute.

Finally, he said, "I don't know what the hell is wrong, but I'll do whatever I can to help. But you have to talk to me. What's this all about?"

CHAPTER NINE

TESS relaxed against Shayde, absorbing his strength. If she were honest with herself, she'd admit she wallowed in it. It wasn't that she really needed someone to lean on. For as long as she could remember, she'd always been the strong one. Others tended to rely on her, and she'd never hesitated to give everything she could to those in need. But for these few minutes, she'd take advantage of what Shayde offered with such unstinting generosity. It felt good. In fact, it felt more than good. It felt wonderful.

Somehow his touch eased the constriction in her throat, allowing her to open up about the most painful experience in her life. "Did you know that in all our conversations, you've never asked how Robert died." Sliding her arms around Shayde's waist, Tess rested her cheek against his chest and clung to him. "Why is that?"

His soft sigh shuddered through her. "I figured if you wanted me to know, you'd tell me."

When had Shayde's gruff voice come to mean so much to her? At some point, it had rumbled its way deep into her pores and lodged close to her heart. "I want you to know."

He pulled back, glancing around the foyer with a frown. "Let's go." He kept one arm folded securely around her. "This isn't the sort of conversation to have out here."

He led her deeper into his apartment, the short hallway

opening into a sprawling living area. Floor to ceiling windows covered one wall and offered an uncomparable view of Puget Sound and the Olympic Mountains. It was still too early for the first dusting of snow and the barren peaks stood out in craggy relief against a crystalline-blue sky. Tess crossed to the windows and allowed the spectacular vista to work its special brand of magic. The tension eased from her muscles and filled her with a hard-won sense of peace.

Shayde joined her at the windows. Cupping her shoulders, he drew her back against his chest. "Talk to me, sweetheart. How did Robert die?"

"It was leukemia."

"Aw, hell." His hold tightened and he lowered his head so his cheek rested close to her temple. He felt good. The scent of him, the heat generated by his body, his soothing touch—all of it enveloped her in a comforting warmth. "That's a rough one."

"Very rough," she concurred, fighting back tears.

"Tell me what happened. How long were you married when the doctors found it?"

The memories were old and distant in some regards, and fresh and painful in others. How quickly life had changed after that one disastrous discovery. She and Robert had gone from being young and carefree to weighing each moment, fighting the passage of every precious second. "We weren't married then. He was diagnosed our senior year in high school."

She'd surprised him. "You knew Robert then?"

"We were best friends most of our lives." She smiled through her tears, remembering those halcyon days of picnics and hikes and childish squabbles. They'd grown from toddlers who'd splashed through mud puddles together to gangly children playing ferocious games of tag to suffering through all the emotional upheavals of an awkward adolescence. And just as they'd teetered on the brink of adulthood, their life had come to a screeching halt. "As we got older, our friendship became something more."

"How did they discover the leukemia?"

She fixed her gaze on the distant mountains, fighting for the balance and serenity the view usually inspired. How many days had she sought out scenery similar to this in the hope it would lessen the agony of those bleak times? Something about the enduring nature of sea and mountain helped calm the storm of rage and bitterness that had threatened to overwhelm her during the darkest years. She drew a deep breath, surprised to discover that Shayde's presence made it easier for her to maintain her composure.

"During high school, Robert's life revolved around baseball. It was his passion. Not only was he our star pitcher, but his teammates unanimously voted him the team captain. About halfway through his final season, he injured his arm during a game. In the course of treating the injury the doctors discovered a lump."

"I'm so sorry, Tess."

"You can't imagine the outpouring of concern from the community. Robert inspired that sort of reaction in people." She glanced over her shoulder. "You'd have liked him, Shayde. He was smart and generous and good-natured."

"You said Gray reminded you of him."

She nodded. "If you and Gray were close enough friends to room together during college, then you can appreciate the sort of man Robert was, even as a teen. He had this quiet fortitude about him." She tilted her head back against Shayde's chest. "Do you know, he went through all those hideous treatments without a single complaint? In fact, he'd go out of his way to encourage the other patients and get them laughing again.''

"When did you marry? After high school?''

She shook her head. "No. We were too young and we both knew it. It wasn't until we were in college. By then Robert's leukemia had gone into remission and we thought he'd licked it.''

"But he hadn't."

"No." That single, bald response said it all.

"When did you decide to marry?''

"At the end of our sophomore year in college." It had been one of the few bright spots during those final months. "We were enjoying this gorgeous, balmy spring day. We'd just completed our last exam and were spread eagle in the grass, thrilled to have finished school for another year. We were young and giddy and high on life. Then Robert rolled over and proposed.''

"Let me guess.'' Shayde's voice sounded rougher than normal, if that were possible. "You said, yes.''

"You're wrong. I think I told him not to be an idiot.'' She glanced up and managed a grin. "Wasn't that romantic of me?''

His expression softened. "I gather you were a practical woman, even in those days.''

"Extremely." Her smile faded. "And then Robert grew serious and said that if he'd learned anything from his illness, it was to live life to the fullest, to seize the moment and squeeze every drop of enjoyment from it. Three hours later we were on a plane for Reno, Nevada. We were married that night.''

"Wedded bliss didn't last long, did it?''

She shook her head. Tears filled her eyes again and she fought them back, struggling to keep her voice steady and dispassionate—not that she fooled Shayde. He turned her into his embrace and caged her within rock-solid arms. It was as though he were silently telling her that no harm would come to her as long as he held her, that he'd do everything within his power to hold her pain at bay.

She rested her cheek against his chest, the steady beat of his heart underscoring his calm strength. ''Right after the fall semester started, we discovered that the cancer had returned. I dropped out of school to take care of him.'' She struggled against the growing thickness in her throat. ''He didn't even make it to Christmas.''

Shayde smoothed his hand back and forth along the length of her spine. ''I'm sorry, Tess. I'm so, so sorry. It must have been horrible.''

''He was such a special person.'' Her tears dampened Shayde's shirt. ''He shouldn't have died.''

''Don't, sweetheart. Don't torture yourself.'' His words contained an underlying urgency, as though he truly had absorbed a portion of her pain. ''Robert had you in his life. That must have made a huge difference to him.''

''I'm glad we married,'' she stated fiercely. ''I'm glad we had that much time together.''

''And I'm sure he felt the same way.'' He waited while she regained control, holding her without speaking. After a few minutes he said, ''I gather Robert's death brings us to your job at Altruistics.''

She nodded. ''And the reason I seem obsessed with gaining my promotion through my own efforts.''

''I assume you went to work there after Robert's death. And that the reason you chose Altruistics is because of all they've done to help find a cure for leukemia.''

"Yes."

"But there's more to it than that, isn't there?"

"Yes," she said again. "A lot more."

"Did you go back to college?"

"No. A week after the funeral, with a mountain of bills to pay, I walked into the offices at Altruistics and filled out a job application." She could still feel the lingering shadows of her long-ago desperation, even after all these years. "Al Portman interviewed me."

"And hired you."

"He hired me instead of a more qualified person."

As usual, Shayde was quick to make the connection. "Because of Robert."

She nodded. "You've got it. Only I hadn't told him about my husband. He found out when he checked my references."

"And ever since then you've been doing everything you can to prove that you're as capable as that other person."

He'd reached the most logical conclusion and she didn't bother denying it. How could she? It was the truth. "If I seem a little zealous in the pursuit of my job, I hope you'll understand."

"Oh, I do understand. All this time you've been worried that Al Portman might have made a mistake and the people who will pay the ultimate price are those Altruistics was designed to benefit."

His words stung, prompting an instant response. "Don't you understand? The job is more important than the person doing it."

Shayde shook his head. "What I understand is that the person currently doing the job is the best one for the position." She'd never heard his voice so tender. "You, more than anyone, realize how vital the work is, how important the contributions are that ensure that work continues.''

''But this woman—''

''May have been eminently qualified. But it's obvious Portman saw something in you he didn't see in this other candidate.'' Shayde gave it a moment's thought. ''If I were to guess, I'd say he saw heart. He saw that you'd put everything you had into the job, that you wouldn't take no for an answer or get discouraged easily. Or have I misjudged your character?''

''I'd do anything—'' Her voice broke and she angrily brushed aside her tears. ''I'd do anything to keep from losing another person the way Robert was lost.''

''Which is what you're going to tell Walt Moore.''

His comment stopped her cold. ''What are you talking about?''

''I'm talking about the third Impossible.'' Steel underscored the compassion she read in his expression. ''He's an Impossible whose wife died of leukemia. You must have read it in his file.''

Tess shook her head. ''I've never capitalized on Robert's death and I don't intend to start now.''

''Capitalize?'' A hint of anger colored the word. ''How about empathize. How about going to the man and letting him know that you know exactly... *exactly*...what he's feeling. That this is a disease that takes young and old, alike, and there's something he can do about that.''

''I don't know if I can talk to him about Robert. Even after all these years, I can barely talk to you about him.''

Shayde clasped her shoulders in a touch of both reassurance and support. ''Then Walt Moore will see that and understand. And if he doesn't, nothing you say will make a difference, anyway.'' His hold tightened. ''But maybe, just maybe, it would help him to know there's something he can do, that his contribution might eventually make a difference for another man's wife."

She didn't think she could go through with it. How could she open up to a complete stranger the way she had to Shayde? It was too personal, too intimate. It cut too close to feelings she'd suppressed for close to a decade.

Once again he read her thoughts. "It's time to share your husband with others, Tess. It's time to put a face on the man who's responsible for your working at Altruistics. You don't need to feel guilty any longer."

Guilty? She pulled free of his arms. "I assume you plan to explain that one?"

Shayde released his breath in a tired sigh. "It's simple, Tess. You survived and Robert didn't. You said it yourself. He was an incredible man. Everyone who knew him, loved him. He didn't deserve to die, not when he had so much to offer."

Every word struck like a blow. "He didn't! He didn't deserve to die."

"And if he'd lived, what would Robert be doing now?"

She froze. "He'd...he'd—"

"Be working for Altruistics? Turning Impossibles with his innate goodness and boyish enthusiasm? He told you that's what he planned to do when he graduated from college, didn't he, Tess? He told you he planned to dedicate his life to finding a cure for the disease that he thought he'd licked. And when it stole him from you, you took up his cause."

His accuracy stunned her and it took three tries to get the words out. "I had to do something to help," she tried to explain. "I couldn't let his dream die with him."

"Of course you couldn't. Don't you get it, Tess? You couldn't because you're every bit as special as Robert. You have the same sort of innate goodness." He tipped her face up to his. "And while I wouldn't describe you as having boyish enthusiasm, you have the sort of feminine passion that moves people to action."

"It might not move Walt Moore," she protested.

"What if it does?"

He was right. As much as she hated to admit it, the time had come to put aside her own pain and do her job. "Okay, I'll make an appointment."

"Somehow I thought you might." Shayde kissed her, the caress filled with barely tempered hunger. "If there's any way I can lend a hand, just ask."

She managed a smile. "Will you catch me when I fall?"

"Always."

The word offered the sweetest of promises, a promise she reveled in. And it offered something else, something she hadn't felt in years.

It offered hope.

"Okay, sweetheart. It's time." Shayde straightened Tess's collar and brushed a fiery ringlet from her brow. "My sources tell me that Walt Moore comes to the park every evening. It's always the same bench, same time, which means he should be along any minute now."

"I doubt he'll appreciate my interrupting his private time," she muttered.

"You're probably right. But I suspect it's the only way you'll get to see him, considering he's turned down all of your other requests." Shayde glanced toward the bench and saw an elderly man approach. "Here he comes. Are you ready?"

"No. But, I won't let that stop me." She lifted her face to his in a gesture as natural as it was appealing. "Wish me luck."

He couldn't resist. He took her in his arms and gave her a kiss of encouragement. If they'd been anywhere else, it would have deepened into something far more, perhaps because Tess had an uncanny knack for putting all of herself into even the simplest of kisses. Or perhaps it had to do with her natural generosity. Or maybe she'd developed an overwhelming hankering for his embrace. Hell, a man could dream.

Reluctantly, he set her free and gave her a gentle nudge in the direction of the park bench. "Good luck, love," he called. "Just be honest with him. That's all anyone can expect."

With a nervous smile, Tess walked away leaving Shayde wishing there were something more he could do to help. Unfortunately, there wasn't. She needed to earn her promotion fairly and he wouldn't interfere with that. She crossed a strip of freshly mowed grass and paused just shy of the park bench where Walt Moore sat. Taking a deep breath, she squared her shoulders and ran her hands along the sides of her slacks. But aside from that one telling gesture, she didn't reveal any hint of nervousness.

The next few minutes were the most crucial. If Tess were allowed to talk, Shayde didn't doubt for a minute that she'd have a good shot at making a case for herself. He leaned against a towering maple and folded his arms across his chest, watching intently.

At first Walt appeared startled by the interruption, then disgruntled. But he didn't object when she sat down beside him. Slowly, the more she talked, the more his demeanor changed. His shoulders sagged in sorrow and he kept shaking his head. But he listened. Nor did he jerk his hand away when she covered it with her own. After an endless ten minutes, the old man stood. He said something to Tess, something that impacted like a slap. And then he walked away.

Shayde didn't wait. He pushed off from the tree and sprinted to her side. She didn't speak, just erupted from the bench and into his arms. "You tried," he murmured against the top of her head. "At least you tried."

"Please take me home."

He didn't hesitate. Within minutes he had her in the Jag, headed for Green Lake. To his concern, she didn't say a word the entire way. Parking outside her house, he followed her inside. "You did your best, Tess."

She slammed the door shut behind her and tossed her purse onto the hallway table. "My best wasn't good enough. Telling him about Robert didn't make the least difference. He told me he'd grieve in his own way, that throwing money at some cause wouldn't bring his wife back."

"He might reconsider once he's had time to think about what you said," Shayde argued. "People listen to you, sweetheart. Even though Walt Moore refused you this time— Hell, even if he refuses you the next time you approach him, he'll still listen to what you have to say. And one of these days you'll get through to him because he'll recognize your sincerity and realize that he wants to act instead of grieve."

His words might have made more of an impact if she didn't feel so utterly defeated. "Thank you for coming with me," she said in her most professional tone of voice. "If you have other plans, I won't keep you any longer."

"That tears it."

Without warning, he swung her into his arms. It never even occurred to Tess to struggle. Instead, she clasped her hands around his neck and held on tight.

"What are you doing?" she asked with impressive calm.

"Catching you." He took her mouth in a swift, passionate kiss that should have added to her tension. To her delight, it did the precise opposite, unraveling her in the most remarkable ways. "Granted, you didn't fall. In fact, it didn't amount to much more than a stumble. But I promised I'd be here for you. And somehow I have the impression you're about to turn into my employer and dismiss me while you lick your wounds in private."

She shot him a teasing look from beneath her lashes. "I gather that's not going to happen?"

His arms tightened around her. "Not a chance. If there's any licking to be done, I'm the man for the job."

"In that case, I have a final order for you."

"And what's that?"

"Take me to my inner sanctum." She waved her hand toward the steps leading to her bedroom. "It's thatta way, in case you've forgotten."

"I haven't forgotten." He lifted an eyebrow. "What am I supposed to do when I get there? Leave?"

She shook her head. "Good heavens, no. You're supposed to make wild, crazed love to me." The words fell somewhere between a demand and a plea.

He got as far as the steps before slowly lowering her to her feet. His arms continued to ring her, but a frown warned that he wasn't exactly swept up in the delirium of the moment. "This isn't a good idea."

"I think it's an excellent idea," she countered.

His frown deepened. "Why are you doing this, Tess? Because you're upset? Lonely? In need of a man?"

"In need of a man, as in any man?" she demanded indignantly. How could he believe such a thing? "Is that what you think?"

"I know you better than that. You're not into casual sex."

She couldn't help laughing. "Are you saying you are?" She tilted her head to one side. "Which is it, Shayde? Are you only interested if it *is* casual...or if it isn't? Or is it that you're not interested at all?"

He pulled her closer. "Does this feel like a man who isn't interested?" He skimmed his hand along the length of her spine, molding her to him. There wasn't any doubt that he wanted her. "Pure physical desire isn't the problem."

"But you want more than just physical, is that it?"

"Yes."

She kept her gaze fixed on his. Direct. Steady. Certain. "So do I."

"Tess—"

Without a word she backed out of his embrace. Unbuttoning her blouse, she stripped it off her shoulders and dropped it to the floor. Next, she reached for the zip at the side of her skirt. The sound of the nylon teeth giving way rent the air.

"What the *hell* are you doing, woman?"

"Settling any remaining questions."

"In the *hallway?*"

"If that's what you want." She inspected the area with mock intentness. "The floor might be a bit hard on your knees, but if you prefer it to the inner sanctum, I can be persuaded."

"That's not what I meant."

"A pity." She allowed her skirt to drop to the floor. Stepping free of it, she started up the steps leading to her bedroom. She paused long enough to glance over her shoulder. "It's your choice, Shayde. You caught me. Now what are you going to do with me?"

"You shouldn't issue challenges, lady."

She didn't bother to reply, but simply added an extra waggle to her hips. She made it to the top of the stairs before he came charging after her. In one smooth movement, he snagged her around the middle and tossed her over his shoulder. Wrapping one arm around her knees, he kicked open her bedroom door.

"Challenging me only accomplishes one thing," he explained kindly.

She viewed her upside down world with a broad smile. "I'm hoping that one thing involves a bed, the two of us and as little clothing as possible."

"You got it."

His hand shifted upward, plying a tantalizing path along the back of her thighs to her silk-covered bottom. His fingers splayed across the rounded curves and it took every ounce of self-possession not to cry out. She bit down on her lip, a dozen different entreaties lodging in her throat. Then she gave up maintaining the least bit of control. Why bother? Shayde should know how he affected her. He should know how desperately she wanted him. She'd spent far too many years hiding from her feelings. But no longer. Shayde deserved total honesty.

"Shayde, please. No more games. Make love to me."

He lowered her to the mattress and regarded her with such a look of tenderness, she wanted to weep. "Are you sure you won't regret this later?"

"I've never been more certain in my life."

The afternoon sun blazed a path across her canopied bed, intensifying the jewel tones of the drapes and spread and pillows. It was as though they found themselves in the midst of a primeval jungle. She'd designed the room to provoke just that sort of reaction. The wildness of form and color spoke to her own inner wildness, evoking emotions she'd refused to allow free rein anywhere else. Inhibitions didn't belong here. Nothing belonged that wasn't open and natural and genuine.

She reached out for him, catching his hand in hers. Tugging, she pulled him onto the mattress to join her. "You have far too many clothes on."

"Then do something about it."

"Ah, a demanding man. I like that."

Setting out to correct the oversight, Tess unbuttoned Shayde's shirt and pushed it from his shoulders. He ripped the shirt the rest of the way off. Planting his arms on either side of her head, his mouth collided with hers. Briefly, their limbs entwined, then released to give them the opportunity to shed more clothing. Her bra joined his shirt. After retrieving a foil packet from his wallet, his trousers followed the other bits and pieces. In the space of a few nervous heartbeats, she removed the last of the barriers separating them and fully bared herself to him.

It was a moment of utter vulnerability and he recognized it almost before she did. "I'm the first, aren't I?"

She didn't pretend to misunderstand. "Since Robert? Yes."

"Why, sweetheart?"

"Because…because you were right." She reached up and slid her fingers through his hair, then traced a path over his angled cheekbones to his mouth. She lingered there, smiling as he buried a kiss in her palm. "All this time I've been afraid of love. And I've been compensating by directing all my focus into my job. It's safer than risking another loss."

"You won't lose me."

"Promise?" It was a cry from the heart.

Stripping the covers from the bed, he settled her into a splash of sunlight and took her into his arms. "I promise, Tess. No matter what happens, I'll always be here for you. I won't leave you. Not ever."

And then he kissed her.

It was a kiss different from all those that had come before. It spoke of an unending need, and of promises made and promises kept. It told of a door closing on the past and opening into the future, and of his desire to be part of that future. It assured her that she'd found someone who'd remain by her side, no matter what that future might bring.

But more, that single kiss revealed a truth she'd been carrying deep in her heart.

Tess stared up at Shayde in wonder. How could she have been so blind? She loved this man. She loved him with a passion she'd never known before. What she'd felt for Robert had been so very different—a first love that had never had the opportunity to mature into something deeper and more permanent. But what she felt for Shayde had blossomed like a flower greedy for sunshine, its roots plunging deep into fertile soil.

"Shayde." His name escaped in a joyful whisper. "Please make love to me."

"I will, sweetheart." He filled his hands with her hair, allowing the curls to cascade through his fingers. Sunshine radiated within the red-gold curls, providing a striking contrast to the paleness of her skin. "Are all the ghosts gone now?"

"All gone," she confirmed. "And they won't be back."

With infinite tenderness he kissed her again, the give

and take of lip and tongue languid and delicious. He didn't rush her, but waited for her desire to build. Not that it took long. Everything about him stirred that desire—the powerful width of his shoulders, the crisp whorls of hair that formed an inverted triangle across his chest, the expression in his eyes whenever he looked at her. Heat washed across her skin and he tracked the gentle burn downward, cupping her breasts and anointing them with his tongue. Not fully satisfied, he followed the wash of heat further, tracing the warmth across her abdomen to the very core of her, where the fire burned with painful intensity. She twisted beneath him, straining her hips upward.

"Easy," he murmured. "Slow and easy."

"I'd rather do it fast and hard. We can try slow and easy next time. Though I doubt it'll work any better."

To her frustration, he didn't listen. Each caress became more tantalizing than the last. His fingertips teased, then soothed, then stroked her with fierce aggression. She was completely open to him, more open than she'd ever been with anyone, ever before. She heard her frantic pleas from a vast distance, heard his incoherent response. Finally, when she couldn't have held on for another instant, he positioned himself between her thighs. In one swift stroke he sank into her fluid softness, then drove into it, shattering her universe and rebuilding it again with that single act of possession. Wrapping herself around him, she matched his rhythm with an instinct that came from the heart and soul. She gave everything she had. And then she gave still more.

His breath exploded close to her ear. She vaguely heard the words he uttered. They must have been life-altering, for instantly, her muscles tensed in reaction and she flew apart, soaring high and far. His response came just as quickly. Her name escaped his lips in a desperate bellow as he followed her over the edge. Hours passed. Or was it minutes? Time had no meaning, only the man who held her safe within their color-strewn world.

At long last she opened her eyes and stared up at him, stared into eyes as pure and steadfast as silver. The ghosts truly were gone and something new and amazing had come in their stead. She'd found what she'd thought she'd least wanted—the sort of happily-ever-after fairy tale she'd wished for her two best friends.

With Shayde she'd found love again.

Shayde escaped the bed. Snagging his trousers from the floor, he climbed into them and silently left the room. Once downstairs, he removed his cell phone from his pocket and punched in a phone number.

"Do you have any idea what time it is?" Shadoe's sleepy voice demanded.

"I quit."

"Shayde?"

"Wake up and listen to what I'm saying, Shadoe. I quit. I won't be your Instigator anymore. Tell the Committee I've officially resigned."

"Let me take a wild stab here...Tess Lonigan is somehow involved in your decision."

"I refuse to set her up with Gray. They're dead wrong for each other."

"And you're right for her?"

"No question."

"You sure?"

"Positive."

"Fine. In that case, she's all yours."

The capitulation came so unexpectedly, it took a minute to switch gears. "Just like that?"

"Just like that," Shadoe confirmed.

Shayde closed his eyes. All the pieces fell into place, the picture becoming an annoying whole and he swore violently. "You set me up, didn't you?"

"Sure did. And I gotta tell you. It worked better than any of us anticipated."

"You will pay, Shadoe."

"Tell it to someone who scares easy."

With an exclamation of disgust, Shayde flipped his phone closed. To hell with his brother and the Committee. As far as he was concerned, they'd simply made his job easier by eliminating one of the problems standing in his way. That left him with one more to handle. Turning, he found Tess standing behind him, wearing his hastily donned shirt. It didn't take a rocket scientist to figure out she'd been there for a while. One look at her expression told him that much.

Okay, so perhaps there were two problems left to handle.

CHAPTER TEN

"YOU'RE an Instigator." Tess's accusation escaped in a low, furious whisper.

"No, I'm *the* Instigator." Shayde scraped a hand across his jaw. "Correction. I *was* the Instigator. I just quit."

She waved that aside as insignificant. "The Committee assigned you to make a match for me?"

"Yes."

"You were supposed to match me with Grayson Shaw?"

He hesitated. "That's a bit complicated," he temporized.

"Why don't you simplify it for me? Or don't you understand simple?" She fired her questions in swift, staccato bursts. "Or is it even more simple than even you're willing to admit...as simple as an inability to understand the concept of truth and honesty?"

She was furious. Full-blown, out of control, gloriously furious. Not that he blamed her. "I was given the job of instigating a romance between you and Grayson Shaw, but—"

"What gives you the right to set me up with anyone?" She stalked deeper into the room, his shirttails fluttering about her thighs. "Why don't we start with that point?"

"What gave you the right to set up your two best friends?" he countered.

That stopped her, causing a momentary discomfort. "They asked me to. Sort of."

He nodded. "That's right. Someone made the initial request. Once it's been made, the Committee investigates the matter and decides whether or not a bit of behind-the-scenes matchmaking is warranted."

"And if it's not?"

"No match."

He could see her fighting exhaustion to put the pieces together. It didn't take long. The second she did, she closed her eyes, exhaustion turning to pain. "Someone has to make the initial request."

"Yes."

She looked at him again, wrapping her arms around her waist. The defensiveness of her stance just about killed him. "Which means someone asked the Committee to find a match for me."

"Yes," he repeated.

"*Who?*"

"Sorry." It would be worth more than his hide to answer that one. "Can't help you there."

"It's Seth, isn't it?"

"Does it matter?"

"No." Her chin wobbled and he couldn't stand still any longer. He started toward her, intent on gathering her in his arms and somehow setting everything right again. It was the wrong move to make. She jerked backward, fury blazing in her eyes. "Don't. Don't touch me."

"Sweetheart—"

"Why did you quit your job with the Committee?" she demanded. "Was it because you slept with me? Am I now a conflict of interest? 'Oops, sorry, fellas. I decided to give into lust instead of setting her up with Prince Charming?'"

The first ripple of anger penetrated his iron control.

"Yes, I quit because of our relationship. Yes, you're a huge conflict of interest. And *yes,* I gave into lust instead of setting you up with Prince Charming, mainly because they'd chosen the wrong prince."

Her eyes narrowed. "What's wrong with Gray?"

"He's not for you."

"I think that's my decision to make."

The ripple of anger spread, intensifying with each passing moment. "You made your decision tonight." His voice sounded as if he were grinding glass between his teeth. "You made it when you took me into your bed."

"I think tonight has proven I made a terrible mistake."

"Don't give me that. You're not attracted to Shaw. You want me and we both know it."

"I happen to think Gray is a very appealing man."

It was the simple truth and it grated more than Shayde would have thought possible. The ripples of anger became waves, snapping his control. "Well, give it up. He's not interested in you."

She stilled. "Now how would you know that?"

Shayde swore beneath his breath. He was making a total hash of this. How was it possible that he could set into motion perfect matches for every other person he'd been assigned, but when it came to his own, he'd managed to all but destroy their relationship. "I apologize. I shouldn't have said that."

"How do you know?"

"I know because he told me there's someone else," Shayde reluctantly admitted. "We're old friends, remember?"

"Did you ask him whether he wanted me? Did you get his permission before taking me to bed?" she demanded. "Is he in on this whole matchmaking scheme of yours?"

"Calm down, Tess." Shayde thrust a hand through his hair. He desperately needed time to figure out how to explain everything to her—without having his head handed to him. One look at Tess warned he wouldn't get that time. "Gray's not in on anything. He didn't know the Committee had selected him for you, any more than you did. And what you don't realize is that—"

"I want my name taken off the list."

"It's already off."

"Thank you." She stepped clear of the doorway. "You can leave now."

He shook his head. "I'm not going anywhere. Not until you listen to me."

"There's nothing left to be said."

"Wrong. There's plenty left to be said."

"I've asked you to leave. Please go."

If her voice hadn't broken on that final word, he'd have continued arguing. Instead, he gave in to her request. "Fine. I'll leave. But just so you know, Grayson Shaw wasn't the Committee's choice. He was a smoke screen."

"Then who...?" Her eyes widened. *"You?* They thought you'd make the perfect prince?"

That stung. "Are you saying I wouldn't?"

She started to reply, then closed her mouth, staring down at her bare toes.

"I'm glad you're willing to admit that much."

Her head jerked up again. "I'm not admitting a thing," she denied.

Shayde fought to maintain a facade of calm, with a touch of logic and reason thrown in for good measure. Tess made that close to impossible. Her hair flamed around her face, every bit as fiery as her anger, while her eyes expressed a bottomless ache that he didn't have a hope in hell of soothing. Everything about her distracted him, providing a stark contrast between her anger and her vulnerability.

Her mouth remained red and swollen from his kisses, the softness in direct opposition to the rebellious tilt of her chin. Her skin was deathly pale, while hot color rode her cheekbones. Even the defiant manner in which her hands closed into fists conflicted with the defenseless way they disappeared beneath the dangling cuffs of his shirt. He wanted to hold her, reassure her, drag her back to bed and use every means at his disposal to explain his betrayal. But it wasn't going to happen that way.

Logic. He'd have to stick to logic and reason, even if the ability to remain calm escaped him. "Why is it acceptable for you to go to the Committee and have them instigate a match on behalf of your friends, but it's not okay for someone who loves you, who has your best interests at heart, to do the same for you?"

"Raine and Emma asked me to do it," she maintained. "I didn't ask anyone to find a man for me."

"That's a load of bull and you know it. You discussed setting each other up when you were a bunch of giggling teens fresh out of high school. A full decade's gone by. Have you checked with them recently?"

Judging by her expression he'd scored a hit with that one. "No," she reluctantly admitted. "I haven't."

"Because they might have stopped you, right?" She couldn't deny it and he pressed home his advantage. "Think about it, sweetheart. How is this matchmaking attempt any different from what you requested for them? If you hadn't overheard my phone conversation, you'd never have known the Committee had taken an interest in you, just as your friends will never know we're instigating romances on their behalf.''

''But I did find out.''

''Yes, you did. And what did the Committee do that was so terrible? They had me throw Grayson Shaw in your path. What happened afterward was up to you.''

''Nothing happened!''

''There's a reason for that.'' He started to reach for her and stopped himself at the last instant. She wouldn't welcome his touch at this juncture and he refused to force himself on her. ''Don't you get it? The choice was always yours, Tess. As it turns out, you rejected Grayson.''

''And chose you, their actual match. And hasn't that worked out just great?'' She backed away from him, her expression closing over. ''Tell your Committee that I'm rejecting their match. You can also tell them not to throw any more Prince Charmings my way. I only need to trip once to know it's time to get off the path.''

''You're making a mistake.''

Her mouth compressed into a stubborn line. ''It's my mistake to make.''

''Dammit, Tess! Are you going to give up on something it's taken you all these years to find again? Are you going to allow fear to win?''

She turned on him, her fury reigniting. ''This isn't fear. It's anger.''

''And you have every right to be angry. But don't let temper drive you to lose out on something unique. I promised I wouldn't leave you and I won't. I'll always be here for you, Tess.''

''You also promised to catch me if I fell.'' She tugged his engagement ring off her finger and held it out.

"What I didn't expect was that you'd be the one to push me."

"I'm also the one who'll break your fall." He could feel her tension escalating and knew she couldn't handle much more. Staying wouldn't help the situation. And it sure as hell wouldn't help Tess. Only one thing would and he resigned himself to that unpalatable fact. He took the ring and pocketed it. "Okay, sweetheart. I'll leave. For now. All this does is put an end to a pretense. The next time my ring hits your finger—and it will hit your finger again—it'll be for the right reasons."

He didn't attempt to touch her. Exiting the room, he took a minute to retrieve the rest of his belongings. He'd make do without his shirt. Somehow he didn't feel like stripping it off Tess as his parting gesture. All the while she remained in the den and he forced himself not to go back in there after her. Leaving the house, he closed the door behind him and stood silently on the porch, waiting. An instant later the dead bolt snicked home in the front door lock.

The symbolism didn't escape his notice.

Shayde drove aimlessly through the darkened streets, the throaty purr of the Jag a soothing accompaniment. He should have told her. The minute he'd decided to stop being an Instigator and go after Tess himself, he should have told her the truth.

So why hadn't he?

He pulled up to a stoplight and stared blindly ahead. A fine rain began to fall, misting the front windshield. The red from the traffic light gleamed within each individual droplet, like dozens of miniature warning beacons. He hadn't told her the truth for one simple reason. He'd been afraid. The irony forced a harsh smile to his

lips. It would seem he and Tess shared a rather unfortunate trait. Just as she'd kept her distance from men out
of fear of loss, he'd kept his silence out of fear that she'd
dump him the instant he told her he worked for the
Committee.

The light turned green and he eased the car into first
gear. A knot formed in the pit of his stomach as he faced
a truth he wanted to deny with every fiber of his being.
There was the strong possibility he wouldn't be able to
fix what had gone wrong in their relationship for one
simple, disastrous reason....

"First, you didn't tell her you were the Instigator, and
then you didn't tell her who you really are," he muttered
beneath his breath. "And that, buddy boy, is what's really going to hang you."

She might have forgiven the first betrayal. But she'd
never forgive the second. He flipped on the wipers as he
ran through his options, the gentle swish combining with
the hiss of tires on wet pavement to play an odd duet.
As far as he could tell, there was only one option available to him—an option that would help her, even if it
didn't help their relationship. He jammed the car into
the next gear. To hell with their relationship. He'd made
a mess of that. The time had come to put her welfare
first. If there wasn't any hope for them, then the least he
could do was ensure she received her promotion.

That decided, he turned the car toward home, the wipers flicking back and forth. "No hope," they droned,
much to his irritation.

"Still hoping," he retorted.

"Come in, Tess." Al Portman greeted her with a broad
grin. "Have a seat."

"Thank you for seeing me." She perched on the edge

of the chair in front of her boss's desk, fighting back a wave of apprehension. "I wanted to update you on a few matters."

"No problem. But first, I'd like to congratulate you on your promotion." He leaned across his desk, holding out his hand. "As of an hour ago you were officially appointed Altruistics newest vice president."

Tess fought to hide her dismay as she shook hands with him. "Should I assume you've received a donation from one of the Impossibles?"

Without a word, Portman flipped open a file centered on his desk and removed a check. He shoved it toward her. "See for yourself."

She read the amount neatly typed in the appropriate space on Gray's bank draft and turned pale. "Very generous."

"We thought so."

"But there's something you should know—"

"Ah, but I'm not finished, yet." He removed another check from the file and deposited it next to Gray's. "Mr. Smith has come through, as well. And his is even more generous than Mr. Shaw's."

Oh, no. This was a disaster. She couldn't let her boss think she'd acquired the money through fair means. Not when she hadn't. "Mr. Portman, before you go any further, I think you should know there's been a conflict of interest in regard to those donations. If you're basing my promotion on these two checks—"

He offered a reassuring smile. "We knew about the conflict of interest. Mr. Smith explained the situation to us and we don't have a problem with it."

She took a deep breath. "But I do."

Portman nodded. "Mr. Smith warned me you'd say that, too."

"Then—"

"And I'd be sympathetic to your dilemma, except for one small detail."

"Which is?"

He removed a final check from the file and set it gently on top of the other two. "This."

The signature at the bottom read Walt Moore. And it was the largest check of the three. "I don't believe it." She released her breath in a long sigh. "He came through."

"He came through because of you, Tess, and the conversation you had with him about Robert. The other two may have contributed because the gentlemen involved were hoping to please you. But Mr. Moore's donation is a result of your hard work and effort, because he feels the cause is just and his money well-spent."

She sagged back against the chair. "I did it."

He chuckled. "Yes, Tess. You did it."

"And…" She moistened her lips. "And Mr. Smith?"

"I think you've found yourself someone very special. I wish you all the best."

Tears pricked her eyes. Not precisely vice presidential behavior, but she couldn't seem to help it. "That may be a little premature."

"I hope not. Tess…" He frowned as he gathered up the checks. "Did you ever wonder why I insisted you turn an Impossible before giving you the promotion?"

"It's not required of all your vice presidents?" she asked lightly.

"No."

Something Shayde said came back to haunt her. "Is it because of Robert? Did you hire me originally so I'd use his death to drum up new business?" The question came out more bluntly than she'd planned. But once asked, she didn't back away from it. "Is that why you picked me over other, more qualified candidates?"

Portman looked shocked. "Absolutely not. If anything, your husband's death gave me pause. I didn't want to hire a zealot. I wanted someone on my staff who could understand the desperation of our need and convey that in a professional, compassionate manner. You were the perfect person for the job."

"I'm sorry." Tess shook her head. "I don't understand. If this wasn't an attempt to get me to use Robert to turn an Impossible, then—"

"Actually, this *is* about Robert." He shifted in his chair, appearing more uncomfortable than she'd have thought possible. "I have to admit it's a bit unprofessional of me."

"Unprofessional?" she teased gently. "You, Mr. Portman?"

"Don't you think it's time you called me, Al?" His smile held an element of compassion. "I asked you to turn an Impossible because I knew it was the only way for you to come to terms with your past. I knew you'd only be able to turn one of the three individuals I'd assigned if you told them about Robert, something you'd never done before with any other client or donor."

"And if I opened up to them about Robert...?"

He gave her a direct look. "It would mean you'd finally put the past where it belonged. In the past. It would also mean that you could judge when it was appropriate to discuss the circumstances surrounding your husband's death with people in need of your empathy. People like Walt Moore. And it would mean you were ready to move forward with your life and with your career. That's the woman I wanted for my next vice president."

"In other words, I'd have stopped trying to make up

for Robert's loss by fulfilling his dreams," she murmured, "and start fulfilling my own. And I'd have stopped being afraid to connect with other people for fear that I'll lose them."

"I apologize, Tess. It wasn't fair of me to put you through that without some sort of explanation. Blame it on an old man watching silently from the sidelines all these years and finally deciding to act, instead of watch. I hope you can forgive me."

"There's nothing to forgive." She gave him a radiant smile. "Mr. Portman...Al? Would you mind if I take the rest of the day off?"

"Going to retrieve your ring?" he asked innocently, glancing at her hand. "I noticed you'd misplaced it."

She touched the bare spot on her finger. "Don't worry. I think I remember where I left it."

He opened the door on the first knock and found Tess standing on his doorstep. He didn't dare react, just in case she turned out to be another dream. "Hello, Shayde," she finally said.

"It's Dick Smith." Okay, that was one way to break the news to her. Probably not the best way, but par for the course, all things considered. "My real name is Dick Smith."

She took the news with amazing equanimity. "Then why do you call yourself Shayde?"

"If you had a handle like Dick Smith, you'd use your middle name, too."

"Tom, Dick and Harry have middle names like Shayde?"

"Shadoe, Shayde and Spirit, to be precise."

He had to hand it to her, unlike most people she didn't so much as snicker. "And Adelaide is your mother."

Tess lifted an eyebrow. "A sixties sort of woman, I assume?"

"She really does love us. She's just—"

"Unique. Yes, I think we've established that." She gestured awkwardly in the direction of his foyer. "Do you think we could talk? Inside, I mean."

Muttering an apology, he stepped out of the way. Oh, yeah. He was batting a thousand now. Give him another few minutes and he'd have the noose wrapped and tied around his own neck. All she'd have to do is slap the horse out from under him. "Can I get you a drink?" he asked, as he led the way to the living room. "Coffee, soda, arsenic?"

She smiled, much to his relief. "No, thanks. I dropped by because I thought you might appreciate an update on the job front."

Uh-oh. Unless he was very much mistaken, that sounded remarkably like a hard slap to a horse's hindquarters. Yes, now that he listened close, he could hear the horse's panicked snort in response. And here it came... A final view of the south end of a fast moving nag while a rope snapped taut around his neck.

He yanked at the tie constricting his throat. "Listen, Tess. You haven't a clue how frustrating it was, knowing that I could ensure your promotion simply by writing a check and not being able to."

"Funny. I believe you did just that."

"Only after you'd ended our relationship," he protested. "Offering a donation to Altruistics was completely fair and aboveboard at that point."

"And only because I wasn't supposed to know Dick Smith was also the mysterious Shayde." She fixed him with an unwavering gaze. "You knew I'd refuse the promotion if I discovered you and Dick were one and the same person, didn't you?''

He cleared his throat. ''The thought did occur to me.''

''So you sacrificed everything in order to make sure I got that promotion.''

''You earned that promotion honestly, Tess. If you'd approached me as a representative of Altruistics, you'd have turned me the second I listened to you talk about your company and about all the people that company helps. I told you before, sweetheart. You have heart. And people feel that. They respond to it.'' He eyed her uncertainly. ''You didn't turn down the promotion, did you?''

''I started to.''

His breathing eased ever so slightly. ''What stopped you?''

''A check from Walt Moore.''

''A check from—'' Shayde gave a shout of triumph and swept her off her feet, twirling her in a dizzying circle. ''You did it. You turned the old reprobate.''

''He's not an old reprobate,'' she protested, holding on for dear life. ''He's a sweet, lonely old man who misses his wife.''

''If it means you got the promotion, I'll nominate him for sainthood.'' He set her on her feet and rubbed his hands together. ''This calls for a celebration. How about champagne?''

''Not just yet.'' She brushed a lock of tousled hair from her face. ''I didn't come just to tell you about my job. There was another reason.''

Aw, hell. ''What reason?''

''I came to ask for your help.''

Help? Was she kidding? He grinned. ''Damn, honey. I do that for a living. Sure. Anything. How can I help?

I'm usually good at it, too, despite current proof to the contrary.'' She took a deep breath, lacing her fingers together in a white-knuckle grip and Shayde frowned. This couldn't be good. "Talk to me, sweetheart. What's wrong?"

"Somewhere along the way, I lost my fiancé," she confessed. "I thought maybe you could help me find him."

It took an instant for her words to sink in. When they did he closed his eyes, his jaw working for a moment. "You didn't lose him," he finally replied, his voice gruffer than ever before. "You just didn't know who he was."

"Actually, I did."

That caught his attention. "You knew I was Dick Smith? When? How?"

"I figured it out the night of the cancer benefit." She tilted her head to one side and reconsidered. "Actually, it was the next morning. Very early the next morning. I woke up in the wee hours and just knew."

"Wait a minute. You were madder than hell when you discovered I was the Instigator, but when you realized I was Dick Smith, you shrugged it off?"

"Somehow one was easier to accept than the other."

He couldn't resist any longer. He gathered her in his arms. To his profound relief, she accepted his touch. She more than accepted it. She melded with him, locking against him like a long-lost piece of himself. "And why is that?"

"Because I loved Dick Smith." She stroked the lop-sided knot in his tie with trembling fingers. "But I was afraid of the Instigator."

Her explanation didn't make any sense. "It's my job

to make sure that fate collides with perfection. What's so frightening about that?''

''It's frightening to me because I wanted what the Committee had to offer.'' The confession came in a low, halting tone. ''I wanted it more than you can possibly imagine and yet I wasn't willing to risk the consequences of loving someone again...of possibly losing that perfect person. That's why I decided to give it to Raine and Emma, instead. If I couldn't have a happily-ever-after romance, maybe they could. Don't you understand?'' She looked up at him, fighting back tears. ''You said it was your job to make sure that fate collided with perfection. You're my perfection.''

''No, sweetheart.'' He swept a thumb along the curve of her cheek, wiping away the dampness. ''That's your role in my life. When I first met you it was my intention to throw Gray in your path in order to see what you did.''

''And if I didn't do anything? If I stepped right over him and kept going?''

''I'd have thrown him a little harder until I was convinced that you really weren't right for each other. But something happened before I could do that.''

''What happened?'

''I fell in love with you.'' He forked his hands deep into her hair. ''Or maybe at that stage it was plain lust. I don't know. All I can tell you is that I started to care. I cared about you as a person. I cared about what happened with your job. Everything about you mattered to me.''

''I fell in love with you, too.''

''And that love scared the hell out of you.''

''Yes.''

''And now?''

She released her breath in a long sigh. "I can continue to be afraid. Or I can grab hold of what I want with both hands."

He smiled tenderly. "Is it my imagination, or are you grabbing me?"

"It's not your imagination. I love you as Shayde. I love you as Dick. And I even love you as the Instigator."

"What if I decide to help out the Committee again?"

"I won't object, so long as you keep making sure fate collides with perfection."

He kissed her then, a kiss of ultimate promise. And she returned that promise with every breath and heartbeat and whispered word. Reaching into his pocket, he removed his grandmother's engagement ring. He'd carried it with him ever since they'd parted, keeping it close as an expression of ultimate hope. Taking her hand in his, he slipped it back onto her finger where it belonged. This time she wore it for the right reason. The only reason.

This time it was for love.

EPILOGUE

SHADOE poured champagne into a pair of crystal flutes and carried them to the sofa. "Congratulations, old girl. You pulled off another one."

"I think I prefer boss lady, if you don't mind," she grumbled.

"Hmm." He handed her one of the glasses and dropped a kiss on her cheek. "Personally, I prefer mother."

Adelaide grinned. "Do you think we should tell your brother the truth?"

Shadoe settled onto the couch and leaned back against the cushions. "Eventually." He took an appreciative sip of his wine. "After the honeymoon, perhaps."

"Or maybe we should wait until he asks for his job back. Playing with all of his investments can get so boring after a while."

"Sounds like hell to me," Shadoe concurred cheerfully.

"And we have Tess's two friends to match. Let's not forget about them. I'm sure your brother will want to help instigate those relationships."

"If only to keep his new bride happy." Shadoe swirled the champagne in the glass, watching as the explosion of bubbles shot a fine mist of wine toward the top of the flute. "So, who's next on the list? Raine or Emma?"

"Oh, Emma, definitely. We can't keep Gray waiting

forever, now can we? He was such a wonderful help instigating the romance between Dick and Tess.''

Shadoe lifted his glass in a salute. ''You're absolutely right. To Emma and Gray.''

''Two of our trickier matches,'' Adelaide murmured, clinking her glass against her son's.

''Trickier?'' He frowned. ''Don't tell me getting those two together could be any worse than Shayde and Tess.''

''Far worse, my dear. But I have an idea.'' She offered her son a mysterious smile. ''I see a whirlwind wedding in their future.''

TO HAVE AND TO HOLD

Marriages meant to last!

They've already said "I do," but what happens
when their promise to love, honor and cherish
is put to the test?

Emotions run high as husbands and wives
discover how precious—and fragile—
their wedding vows are....
Will true love keep them together—forever?

Look out in Harlequin Romance® for:

HUSBAND FOR A YEAR
Rebecca Winters (August, #3665)

THE MARRIAGE TEST
Barbara McMahon (September, #3669)

HIS TROPHY WIFE
Leigh Michaels (October, #3672)

THE WEDDING DEAL
Janelle Denison (November, #3678)

PART-TIME MARRIAGE
Jessica Steele (December, #3680)

Available wherever Harlequin books are sold.

HARLEQUIN®
Makes any time special ®

THE AUSTRALIANS

MEN WHO TURN YOUR WHOLE WORLD UPSIDE DOWN!

Look out for novels about the Wonder from Down Under—where spirited women win the hearts of Australia's most eligible men.

Harlequin Romance®:

OUTBACK WITH THE BOSS
Barbara Hannay (September, #3670)

MASTER OF MARAMBA
Margaret Way (October, #3671)

OUTBACK FIRE
Margaret Way (December, #3678)

Harlequin Presents®:

A QUESTION OF MARRIAGE
Lindsay Armstrong (October, #2208)

FUGITIVE BRIDE
Miranda Lee (November, #2212)

Available wherever Harlequin books are sold.

HARLEQUIN®
Makes any time special®

What happens when you suddenly
discover your happy twosome is about
to be turned into a...*family?*
Do you laugh?
Do you cry?
Or...do you get married?

The answer is all of the above—and plenty more!

Share the laughter and the tears with
Harlequin Romance® as these
unsuspecting couples have to be

When parenthood takes you by surprise!

THE BACHELOR'S BABY
Liz Fielding (August, #3666)

CLAIMING HIS BABY
Rebecca Winters (October, #3673)

HER HIRED HUSBAND
Renee Roszel (December, #3681)

Available wherever Harlequin books are sold.

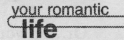